Meanicures

meanicures

catherine clark

EGMONT
USA
NEW YORK

EGMONT

We bring stories to life

First published by Egmont USA, 2010
443 Park Avenue South, Suite 806
New York, NY 10016

1 3 5 7 9 8 6 4 2

www.egmontusa.com
www.catherineclark.com

Library of Congress Cataloging-in-Publication Data

Clark, Catherine.
Meanicures / Catherine Clark.
p. cm.
Summary: Maine seventh-grader Madison and her two best friends, who are being mocked and belittled by former members of their group, decide to conduct a ritual to purge their tormentors from their lives, with unexpected results.
ISBN 978-1-60684-100-6
[1. High schools–Fiction. 2. Cliques (Sociology)–Fiction. 3. Friendship–Fiction. 4. Schools–Fiction. 5. Maine–Fiction.] I. Title.
PZ7.C5412Me 2010
[Fic]–dc22
2010011313

Book design by TME

Printed in the United States of America

CPSIA tracking label information:
Random House Production • 1745 Broadway • New York, NY 10019

For Amy Baum

First Things First

Don't look at me like that.

No, really, please don't, because I'm having a bad hair day. And, speaking as the daughter of Maine's number one all-natural, organic, chemical-free hair product queen, I would know. In fact, I know more about bad hair days than the average twelve-year-old should *ever* know.

Still, don't look at me and act all judgmental. So what if it was my idea to try to get the mean girls out of our lives? Can you blame me? Much?

The thing about Cassidy, Alexis, and Kayley was this: in fifth grade we were friends. Even when we moved to middle school in sixth grade, we still did lots together and stayed close.

But then this year?

Ever since the start of seventh grade, Cassidy, Alexis, and Kayley hadn't talked to us very much, and when they did, they usually made fun of us.

They acted like we'd never all been in Girl Scouts together, or gone on that horrid overnight camping trip where we nearly got devoured by blackflies.

Like we'd never all signed up for a 10K charity walk because they were handing out giant chocolate chip cookies to anyone who enrolled the day of the event, and then suffered our way through it with major blisters because we didn't have the right shoes.

Like we'd never sung Christmas carols outside in a hailstorm, because our music teacher thought it would help us build character.

We felt these things had bonded us—or at least me, Taylor, and Olivia—for life. I guess the others didn't feel that way.

The mean girls weren't just *done* with us, though. It wasn't just that they acted like all those things had never happened. They acted as if they were better than us, and it was their job to keep reminding us of that fact.

Well, we couldn't just sit there and *take* it. Could we?

Chapter 1

I should have been suspicious from the start. I don't do well on Mondays. None of us do.

Olivia dreaded Mondays so much she had started wearing her days of the week underwear in the wrong order, to try to skip over the day completely.

Too much information? Sorry.

Honestly, though, she was so spacey that I'd be surprised if she *ever* wore the correct day. (That's why I sometimes called her "Oblivia.")

Taylor and I had just arrived at school, and just like we did every day, we locked our bikes to the rack outside the west entrance.

But unlike every day, I dropped my key ring into the mud. When I bent to pick it up, the knees of my jeans and my sneakers got muddy.

You could say that it was not a good omen. We have a lot of mud here in Payneston, because it rains way too often, but I'm usually fairly coordinated. I even used to take ballet, and in sixth grade and for a couple of weeks of seventh I was on the school cheerleading and dance team.

I took off my helmet, shook out my long hair, and glanced at the crowd assembled on the sidewalk in front of school. It was about eight forty-five, and classes didn't start until nine.

"Here comes Cassidy," Taylor warned me.

I glanced up from cleaning my keys on the wet grass to see my former BFF, Cassidy, and my other former friends, Alexis and Kayley, headed toward us. They were dressed like clones, in low-cut jeans faded to the same exact shade, matching hoodies in different colors, and Converse sneakers. Cassidy's long blond hair was swinging from side to side as she walked. She looked so happy and perfect, like she was on the front of a catalog or something.

I looked down at my own outfit, feeling self-conscious about my skinny-leg jeans, corduroy jacket, T-shirt, and chunky black shoes. Why was I trying to be different? "Of course. It's Monday, and I'm muddy," I said. "They're coming over to make fun of me. What else can go wrong?"

"I'm not afraid of her," said Taylor. It's fine for her to say that. Anyone brave enough to hurtle over a vault, or leap while on a balance beam, has to be strong, even if she is the size of a fourth grader. Before school, I'd swung by Taylor's house, the way I did every morning until winter came and it was too cold to ride. Taylor rode her bike like she did the uneven bars. Very, very riskily. I usually struggled to keep up with her.

She and Kayley trained and competed on the same

4

club team at the Mainely Gymnastics Center. They used to be such good friends, and they were both so talented, that people referred to them as Team Tay-Kay. You know, one of those cute nicknames that follow athletes all the way to the Olympic Games?

We had this minivan caravan that went to gymnastics meets, with TEAM TAY-KAY written in white shoe polish on the windows. Only, Team Tay-Kay didn't exist anymore. Now, as soon as a meet was over, they took off in opposite directions. Now there was Team Taylor And Team Kayley.

We didn't only travel to gymnastics meets. There were trips to Portland for dance team and cheer camp—me, Cassidy, and Alexis. Silly overnights in hotels, staying up late to watch movies and trying to sneak around the hallways (our moms always caught us because we laughed too loudly).

Olivia mostly only took trips to the Humane Society to adopt new pets, but that wasn't a sport. We'd go along, mostly to look at the cute kittens. I desperately wanted one.

I'd dropped out of cheer earlier this fall. I just wasn't all that interested in it anymore. Dance didn't start again until winter and I wasn't sure whether I'd try out for that, either.

So much had changed in such a short time.

"Madison?" Taylor said as the other girls walked up. "Your hair—"

"Looks very interesting this morning," Cassidy said.

"I know, I know. I have helmet hair." I ruffled my hair with my fingers, trying to make it less flat. Why did Taylor never have this problem?

"Well, don't sweat it, that happens to everyone," said Alexis, giving me a strange look. She was half Japanese and half African American, and she had gorgeous light brown skin and curly hair. She seemed to be able to wear any color and look good in it.

Me? I was the opposite. I had strawberry-blond hair and pale, freckled skin. Alexis and I were the same height, though—five foot five—which worked really well when we made pyramids.

"I mean, it's just great you still ride your bike to school," Alexis said in an "aren't you cute" tone.

"It's good for the environment," I said. Living with an organic fanatic, I'd had enough drilled into me about the environment to last a lifetime. A couple of lifetimes.

"Um, Madison, you want my hat?" offered Taylor. "I think I have a hat in here. . . ." She was rummaging through her backpack.

"Okay, okay, enough about helmet hair, Madison. I've got good news for you," said Cassidy. "*Great* news, actually."

"You have good news," I repeated. "For me. Seriously?" Maybe Cassidy, Alexis, and Kayley had decided to transfer to St. Ignatius Academy, on the other side of town. Maybe their parents had all gotten new jobs in, say, Singapore. Was that far enough away?

"Well, *yeah*," Cassidy said with a laugh, like wasn't I

being ridiculous. "You're *not* going to believe this. We were just talking with Hunter Matthews."

"Right . . ." I said slowly.

"You know how you used to have a crush on him, right?" asked Cassidy.

I hated that "we used to tell each other everything" stuff. "What? I did not," I said.

"You did, too!" said Taylor.

I glared at her. How was she helping?

"Hunter totally wants to ask you something," said Cassidy.

"Yeah, right." I glanced over at Hunter, who was sitting on the brick wall, fiddling with his cell phone. Hunter wasn't exactly a friend. In fact, he was an eighth grader who rarely said hello to me. I sat in front of him in algebra, a class that was mostly for eighth graders and a few seventh graders like me. Hunter usually did obnoxious things like breathe extra-hotly on my neck because I'd once asked him not to, so now he knew it annoyed me. He once told me that I looked like a hedgehog when I dressed in a brown fuzzy sweater (which *was* rather hideous, now that I think about it).

You know how sometimes you just really, really want to believe something? And so you do? "Seriously? He wants to ask me something?" I asked.

"Oh, yeah. He said something about the eighth-grade dance!" Kayley said.

What? Me? *Me?* I'd never been asked to any dance before. I looked at Taylor. "Should I?"

"I don't know," she said softly. "If you want . . ." She shrugged.

I was feeling brave. Don't ask why, because I don't know. These flashes of bravery come to me from time to time, like lightning strikes. What if it was true and I didn't act on it?

I walked slowly toward Hunter and stopped in front of him. "Um, hi. I heard you might talk to me? *Want* to talk to me, I mean."

He was still texting and he didn't look up. "Yeah. Just a sec."

I waited a couple of seconds. Then I said, "Hunter?"

"Just a sec," he said again.

He wasn't good at math. He probably had no idea what "a second" even meant. I was too impatient and curious to wait another minute. "If you were going to ask, um, the answer's yes."

He finally looked up and stared at me blankly, his sandy-brown hair falling into his hazel eyes.

"The dance," I said. "Yes."

"Yeah? Cool. See, I can't go to the dance unless I get a C in math. I can't even play in the football game *before* the dance if I don't get a C. So I can borrow your homework?" he asked.

"Huh?"

"That was what I needed to know," he said. "You *said* yes. I'll give it back after homeroom."

Math homework. He wanted to cheat off my math homework, not ask me to the dance. Of course.

"Um . . ." I sorted through my backpack, trying not to show him how embarrassed I was for getting things wrong.

"What happened to your hair?" he asked. "Looks green. Sort of like seaweed? You might want to get that checked out."

He just compared my hair to seaweed. I wanted to grab Hunter's phone to call my mom right then. I would tell her: *I am no longer willing to be a test subject, and I think your seaweed shampoo recipes are full of salt and a lack of scientific knowledge, and do you realize you're the reason I will never, ever have a date?*

I just smiled at Hunter. "It's a long story," I said. A long, long, pathetic story. I handed him my math homework and walked away—bumping right into Alexis, who was taking our picture.

"Why are you taking my picture?" I asked.

"It's candids for the yearbook—we're taking them of everyone. Go back and stand next to Hunter," she said.

"No, thanks—" I started to say, but she had already snapped the photo.

"Perfect!"

I slunk away, wishing I were invisible, along with my helmet head and green hair.

"So? What did he *say*?" Cassidy asked eagerly, stepping in front of me.

I stared at her with a blank expression. "He said my hair looked like seaweed."

"Ouch." Cassidy's mouth twitched as though it was killing her not to giggle.

Silently I cursed my mother again, using all the bad words I knew she'd ground me for saying. How had I not noticed this before I left home? How had she not mentioned it? You'd think my little brother would have had a field day.

"You guys could have said something," I said angrily.

"I tried—" Taylor began.

"I just thought you were, you know." Cassidy grinned. "Trying to show your Panther pride."

"How so?" I said.

"Green's one of our school colors, right?" said Alexis.

"You know, you really need to have a talk with your mother about this sham*poo* stuff," Kayley commented, with the emphasis on *poo*.

"Yes. I know," I said through gritted teeth. "I'm well . . . aware of that."

I suddenly saw Olivia walking toward us. She was wearing her usual funky attire: two-toned Converse sneakers, black skirt over striped tights, and jean jacket. Her wavy brown hair was pulled up in a beaded barrette. She was carrying a little pad of paper in one hand, and a pen in the other, and I suddenly got nervous on her behalf. If she was planning on writing things down, that must mean she wasn't comfortable talking.

She had just gotten braces on Saturday, and I wondered how much the mean girls would make fun of her. She had to wear this thing called a pendulum appliance, which made her talk funny because she wasn't used to it yet.

"Don't you have someplace else to go?" I asked Cassidy, hoping she'd leave before she got a chance to hear Olivia try to speak. "Some other person's morning to wreck?"

"Yu mnpf dot wck," said Olivia. "Munez."

The mean girls stared at her, smiles widening on their faces.

"*What* did you just say?" Alexis asked her.

Cassidy laughed. "Yeah, what happened to you?"

"They're called braces. Everyone's heard of them. Come on, guys." Taylor took both of us by the arms and started to pull us away, into the school building.

Olivia quickly scribbled something on a piece of paper and held it up for us to read. *I knew I should have worn my Wednesday underwear!*

Chapter 2

"You have to help me!" Olivia pleaded a minute later, as soon as we were alone in the girls' bathroom on the second floor. Her speech was still indistinct, but I could figure out what she was saying.

"Help you? Look at me!" I cried. Now that I could see my hair in the mirror, I was cringing. All I can say was, my mom was not even close to figuring out the new edamame formula she was experimenting with for her Edamommy Baby Shampoo.

She usually hires hair models to try out new formulas on, but every once in a while she'll get inspired and it'll be the middle of the weekend, and so I become her test subject. Thank goodness, the seaweed shampoo recipe was perfect now. But you know those no-animal-testing symbols on shampoo? I'd like to have one that says: "No Madison Testing."

Still, I have to admire her. I go into a drugstore and look at all the shampoos and conditioners on the shelves, and I think, *It's all been done, Mom.*

She doesn't see it that way. She's made a million with her Original Sea Clean products. She even bought a big house for us *by* the sea. So who was I to question her when she said she wanted to try making edamame baby shampoo?

But obviously, I should have questioned her. In case you don't know, edamames are green vegetables, kind of like peas.

"Couldn't that be the green paint in here reflecting off my hair? Or the fluorescent light, maybe?" I asked.

"Sorry," said Taylor. "But no."

I sighed. "Why didn't you tell me?"

"You had your helmet on until we got here—I didn't know!" said Taylor. "And I tried to get you to wear my hat, didn't I?"

I tried arranging my hair to hide the green streak. The problem was, there wasn't just one. The streaks blended into one another. I quickly pulled my hair into two braids and flattened them down. It wasn't stylish, and I looked like a green Pippi Longstocking, but it was better than before. I pulled Taylor's black Mainely Gymnastics cap over my head to complete the look. Nerdy, but safe.

"Okay, that's better. Now, what do you need help with?" I asked Olivia as we walked out into the hallway, toward our lockers.

In spite of the braces, she managed to get out that today was the day she was scheduled to host "Panthers Update," our school's TV morning news. For some reason the Payneston powers-that-be had decided that every student should host one morning each school year. Not just those who wanted to, but also those who *didn't* want to, who would rather run screaming from the building and get hit by a bus than be on camera.

Like Olivia. Normally she loved being dramatic, and she didn't mind any extra attention that she earned with her brightly colored, offbeat shoes or clothes. But not this Monday, not now when she couldn't speak straight.

"I hate to point out the obvious, but since you knew you were getting braces on Saturday, why didn't you just reschedule it?" Taylor asked as she stacked her science book onto her math book. Taylor's the queen of logic and can never understand why everyone else doesn't act as rationally as she does. When she found out she was sneezing all the time because of her new puppy, she decided she'd just have to give him away— to Olivia, who kept about eight different pets. She didn't even shed a tear.

Olivia shrugged. "I forgot?"

She really can be such a space cadet. Sometimes she'll forget what class she's supposed to go to, or head down the wrong hallway to her locker. You have to take pity on her. It's like she's spending all her brain energy caring for her guinea pig, rabbit, hamster, ferret, three cats, one newly adopted-from-Taylor puppy, and one older dog. She wants to be a veterinarian when she grows up, but I don't know if I'd trust her with surgery. She might be the type to leave important surgical stuff inside your pet—like scissors.

Olivia handed me a piece of paper. *Come on, Madison. I can't talk. Please, can you do it instead? I already went in and cleared it with Mr. Brooks.*

"*Me?*" Pity was one thing. Insanity was another. "No. You can do it. Practice talking! You know, 'Four-score and seven years ago, our fathers . . .' all that kind of stuff."

"'She sells seashells by the seashore,'" I added, though frankly, I'd never seen anyone ever selling seashells, by the seashore or anywhere else.

Olivia tried to say something and sprayed me with spit. It sounded like . . . well . . . like a sailboat slicing through the water.

I realized how dire her situation was. I might be teased if my green hair was picked up on camera, but she'd get laughed off the screen. "Okay, fine. You're not doing it," I said. "But why should *I* do it?"

She handed me another note: *Don't forget to mention the Endangered Animals Club meeting after school today.* Then she pushed me toward the TV studio door, spitting something about how I was good in a crisis.

"No, I'm not!" I said. "Taylor's the one who—"

The door closed. I brushed the spit off my corduroy jacket as Mr. Brooks, who ran the studio, explained how things would work. It seemed straightforward enough—I would read the news while looking at the camera, make eye contact with the camera, smile for the camera, and enunciate (to the camera, no doubt).

"Enunciate. E-nun-ci-ate," Mr. Brooks said. "You

know, like in *My Fair Lady*. Quickly. Quickly!" He seemed to be panicking and saying everything twice because of it. "The rain in Spain stays mainly in the plain. You know, like that. Five minutes till airtime, everybody! Cameron's running the camera, Cassidy's our director—if you need anything, just ask Cassidy."

Just ask Cassidy? I'd rather gargle with glass. Since when did Cassidy take over the morning news?

It figured, though. She'd always wanted to be either an actor or a news anchor, which I think she'd be perfect for, considering she already knows how to act fake all the time. And she was great at cheerleading—a natural performer.

"Um, where is she, anyway?" I asked Cameron. He was also in seventh grade, but I didn't know him very well. His one distinguishing feature was that he looked kind of like the actor in those vampire movies. I mean, the werewolf dude.

He shrugged. "Late, as usual," he said.

"You can't wear that hat, though, Madison," Mr. Brooks said, pointing to Taylor's hat. "You must know the dress code: no hats in school."

"Mr. Brooks, please! I *need* to wear a hat. My hair is, uh, off-color," I said.

He raised his eyebrows. "Off-color? What do you mean by that?"

"It's—not right," I said. "Turned green last night." I slowly removed the hat.

"I'll say," added Cameron, looking closely at me.

I frowned at him. Go ahead, kick me while I'm down. Maybe I *didn't* want to know him better.

Mr. Brooks shrugged. "I don't know what you're talking about. You're being too sensitive. Looks fine to me. No hats."

Cassidy breezed through the door just then. "Hey, Cam, hey, Mr. Brooks," she said with a wave. "*So* sorry I'm late. The printer was not working at all." She stopped and did a double take. "Madison? What are you doing here? Olivia was signed up for today."

"She's not feeling well," I said. That, and she can't talk, I added silently.

"Oh. Well, you know the routine, right? Okay, I have your text all ready, right here." She waved a couple of sheets of paper in the air, then handed them to me. "Do you need anything before you go on? I mean, I know how you hate doing makeup, right? If you want, I could help."

I glared at her. Would a mouse accept help from a snake? Even if the mouse did look . . . a little mousy and green and in no way ready for her close-up.

And what was with her saying she knew I didn't like makeup? Was that a slam?

"No. That's okay." I coughed, wondering if she might actually be offering something good for a change. "Do people usually wear makeup when they do this?"

"Not everyone, but if you want to look good . . ." She paused, waiting for my answer.

"Okay, I guess," I said. "But what are we talking about?"

"Just a quick brush with some powder. Really takes the shine off."

"What shine?" I asked.

"The camera. It tends to make people's faces look shiny."

"Don't I want to be . . . shiny?" I asked. "Sparkly? Happy?"

"Sure. But not *oily*," she said as if my face were no different from the bottom of a pizza box. She sat me down and went to work.

"Two minutes, people, two minutes!" called Mr. Brooks. You would have thought he was directing a big play instead of a one-person teensy-tiny newscast with one video camera.

The thing is, I didn't have oily skin. One of the gifts of my mom's experimentation was that I usually had clear, not-so-bad skin. I figured it was due to the extreme aloe and cucumber exposure I suffered as a young child: the Green & Clean Shampoo year.

"This looks great, Madison!" Cassidy stepped back to admire her work. "Now, maybe a little lip gloss?" she suggested.

I hated her superior attitude. So I didn't normally wear lip gloss. So what?

But if it would get her to stop hounding me, fine. "Sure. Okay." Maybe it would distract from the cursed green hair. I borrowed her gloss, rolled some onto my finger, then applied it to my lips. It couldn't hurt to have a little color. At least, that's what magazines always said.

As I took my seat in front of the camera, Cassidy adjusted the overhead light so that it was pointed directly at my face. "Um, are you sure the light's supposed to be *that* bright?" I asked.

"Oh, yeah," she said. "It'll make you totally pop on camera."

"Pop? Like popcorn? It does feel hot."

"I know, isn't it a pain? Don't worry," Cassidy said, "you'll be fine."

I straightened my shirt and tried to sit up straight. My mom's done several TV appearances and she's always telling me how important it is not to slouch, how it makes you look small and unimportant. (She has a media consultant for stuff like this.)

My mouth suddenly felt completely dry. I ran my tongue over my teeth. Mr. Brooks had said to "enunciate," like in *My Fair Lady*. If anyone knew that musical, it was me. Mom used to watch it all the time, and she'd almost named me Audrey, after the actress in the movie version, Audrey Hepburn. Instead, she named me Madison after . . . well . . . a street.

"The rrrrrain in Maine stays mainly in Payneston," I trilled in a singsong voice. "The rrrrrain in Mmmmaine stays mmmmainly in Payyyyneston."

"Madison, you're on," Cassidy whispered.

"Sorry?"

"You're *on*. Live," she said.

"I am?" I coughed. "Ah—in—in this morning's news," I stuttered the typed announcements Cassidy had given me. "Oh, yes. Well. Just a second here . . . I mean, uh, good morning." I grabbed the two sheets of paper and read, "Happy Tuesday, Panthers!"

Wait a minute, I thought. *That's not right.*

"Excuse me, Monday. Panthers. We're Monday Panthers." I coughed. This wasn't off to a good start—if it was off to a start at all. "Roar your Panther selves to the library this week and learn all about Maine's history, in honor of Postal Heritage Days."

I stopped. We weren't known for our postage. Who had written this?

"Excuse me. Coastal. Coastal Heritage Days," I corrected myself, squinting at the page.

I glanced over at Cassidy. She was smiling and signaling me to continue.

"In other related news, the middle school Council is meeting to discuss why we're called Panthers, when we live at the coast. Was *lobster* already taken?" I cleared my throat. "And if so, how do we get it back?"

I paused, contemplating this. Kind of a deep question for the PMSC, in my opinion. I didn't think they'd be able to handle it. I didn't know I'd be reading jokes. Was today Payneston Comedy Day?

"Moving on . . . From the drama department, for anyone who wants to sing up"—I coughed—"*sign* up for holiday chorus, auditions will be held immediately after tryouts for the winter play, *Our Towel*."

"Town!" Mr. Brooks yelled. *"Our Town!"*

"Right, that's *Our Town*," I said. "Not our . . . towel. That would be a really, um, bad play." I wondered if Cassidy had typed this up herself. And if she had, were her mistakes on purpose? This was going in such a disastrous direction, I had to steer it back toward something positive. I remembered the note Olivia had given me.

"While I have the floor. The mic, whatever. This afternoon is the first meeting of the new Endangered Animals Club, at three o'clock in the after-school club room. The club will be trying to raise money to donate to organizations devoted to saving the animals of the world who are, um, endangered. And we'll be trying to save them," I said, feeling like I was stumbling over every word. "Olivia Salinas and I are in charge of the committee this year, and everyone's welcome—the more, the merrier. So put that on your calendar and get ready to, um, be—I mean, help—an endangered species." I coughed.

The way Mr. Brooks was glaring at me from the audio booth, I was starting to feel semi-endangered myself. I guessed we weren't allowed to promote our own causes. I went back to the prepared—poorly prepared—text from Cassidy, hating every word of it.

"The Chest Club would like to announce that they competed in the first-ever southern Maine—" I stopped. "Chess Club. That's Chess Club. And they competed in the southern Maine championships and came in, uh, what's this . . . ninth place. Out of nine teams. Way to go, Chest—Chess Club." I took a deep breath. This was like a nightmare I'd once had. Only worse.

"Also today," I went on, "please stop by the band office to support the marching band during their candy sale. Chocolate bras are available—excuse me. Candy *bars*. *Bars*. Made of chocolate."

I could hear laughter coming through the floor, echoing in the hallways. The entire school was laughing. At *me*.

"I'd like to finish with today's reflection," I said, thinking, scanning the four-line poem that ended the typed newscast. *Why not? This is a train wreck anyway. Might as well toss a caboose on the end and smash that, too*. I read aloud, "Dead lobsters are red, live lobsters are green. This was probably the worst newscast that you've ever seen."

Cassidy started to applaud, while Cameron shut off the camera and backed away from me as if I were slightly radioactive.

Chapter 3

"Great job!" Cassidy said with her most insincere smile ever—which was saying a lot, for her.

"How could you do that to me?" I cried.

"What do you mean?" She just kept grinning, like that weird Cheshire cat in *Alice in Wonderland* that always gave me the creeps. "I didn't do anything."

I glared at her. "Either you are a lousy proofreader who doesn't know how to write, or you thought it'd be funny to embarrass me—and everyone else with a chest—by making really bad jokes."

"You have a chest?" she said.

I was speechless. She'd sabotaged me. Out-and-out sabotaged me. There were a hundred things I wanted to say, like:

1. I can't believe you set me up like that. I bet you didn't do it alone, either.

2. Why would you do that?

3. Didn't we used to be friends?

4. Remember the time your mouth was on fire and I put it out?

It's a long story, but once in fifth grade we were at Girl Scout camp, making s'mores. Cassidy went to blow out her burning marshmallow and the flames somehow jumped to her lips. I noticed she needed help and put my arm across her mouth, smothering the fire, and saving her life. But apparently, that didn't count for anything anymore.

Mr. Brooks hurried over, a concerned expression on his face. "Uh, Madison, we'll need to talk about this," he said as I walked toward the door.

"Maybe you should talk to her," I said, pointing at Cassidy.

"Me?" Cassidy asked. "What did I do?"

"Look at this—" I started to show Mr. Brooks the text she'd given me, but she grabbed the paper out of my hands before he could see it.

"I'm so sorry, Mr. Brooks. I should have warned you. She's been *really* stressed out lately. I don't know *what* happened," Cassidy said.

I glared at her again, trying to shoot daggers with my eyes.

"Uh, your skin's all red—are you having an allergic reaction to something in here?" asked Cameron.

"It's called embarrassment," I said as the bell rang, ending homeroom. I dashed out into the crowded hallway, jamming Taylor's hat back onto my head, and nearly ran right into Hunter.

"The rrrrrain in Mmmmmaine . . . ," Hunter said, shoving my homework back at me without slowing

24

down. Then suddenly he stopped. "Hey. I didn't know the circus was in town."

"What?" I said.

Taylor and Olivia skidded around the corner just then, grabbing me and pulling me down the hallway. "What happened to your face?" asked Taylor.

"I don't know. Why?"

"It's all red!" Olivia said, still sounding muffled, but not as bad as she'd sounded earlier.

"It was Cassidy. She wanted to do my makeup." I said.

"Well, she did it, all right." Taylor pulled me along even faster.

"Hey! Green hair!" someone yelled from down the hall.

"Don't go postal!" another person called as we ducked into the bathroom for the second time that morning.

I just stood there with my eyes closed, while Olivia got a wet paper towel and gently washed the red off my face. I didn't look at my reflection. I couldn't.

"Loogkon da beefsight," Olivia said. "It cowf bin *e*. Oof shave *e*."

I translated: "Look on the bright side. It could have been *me*. You saved *me*."

She had a point. Maybe there was something to be said for saving a friend. Maybe all I'd remember a year from now would be the fact that I'd taken a bullet for Olivia. She'd never forget this kind of sacrifice. And I, well, I'd be kind of a legend for being so nice.

But as we walked out of the bathroom to hurry toward our first-period classes, two boys walked by holding sheets of paper that said WE ❤ CHOCOLATE BRAS!

Or, then again, maybe I'd just be a legend for other reasons.

"Never mind them," said Taylor. She took my arm and guided me down the hall. "And don't look at who's coming our way."

I don't know about you, but when somebody says to me, "Don't look!" I just have to look. So I did.

Then I wished I hadn't, not that it would have changed anything.

"The rrrrrrain in Mmmmaine . . . ," Alexis was trilling as she came closer.

"Falls mainly on P-p-p-p . . ." Kayley was laughing so hard she couldn't finish the sentence.

What did I say? We didn't do well on Mondays. The mean girls did. I slunk into my first-period class, avoiding the looks that came my way and wondering if I could talk my mom into a quick trip to Paris. Say, tomorrow?

Then again, it was my mom who'd gotten me into this mess. I shuddered and jammed Taylor's hat farther down on my head.

"Do you think anyone else is coming?" I asked Olivia at about three fifteen that afternoon. We had the after-school Endangered Animals Club meeting to ourselves. We had handouts nobody wanted. We had sign-up sheets that were totally blank. I wished Taylor was with us, but she had gymnastics.

"Sure. Maybe they just didn't get the time right," she said.

"Maybe I said the wrong time?" I asked.

Olivia shook her head. "You didn't."

"Maybe I said the wrong room?" I asked.

"You didn't," Olivia said again, doodling on the blank sign-up sheet. "Anyway, there's only one club room."

"True," I mused. "Maybe they don't want to be in a club with a clown?" I suggested.

Why did I agree to start this club with Olivia, anyway? She was the animal lover, the queen of pets, and rescuer of abandoned creatures. I just had a crazy cat named Rudy.

I sat down at the table and put my head in my hands. "What if you created a club and nobody joined?" I wondered out loud.

Olivia leaned back in her chair and put her feet up on the table. "Nobody's coming, are they?"

"We'll have to get things started on our own," I declared. I was determined not to fail at everything today. "So what is this club of ours going to do, exactly?"

"I was thinking we could have a couple of bake sales?" said Olivia. "You know, that's what everyone else does."

"Sure, if they want to make ten dollars. That's not enough. What else?"

"Uh, sell T-shirts?" she suggested.

"What T-shirts?" I asked.

"The ones we're going to design—well, you are. I figured with your design background . . ."

"What? I don't have a design background," I said.

"Your mom does. Anyway, we'll figure that out at our second meeting," said Olivia. "When more people are here."

I heard laughter echoing in the hallway. "Hey, someone's coming!" I said to Olivia. "Look natural."

"Natural?"

"Casual, like, we didn't expect anyone until now," I said.

The laughter came nearer.

Suddenly, the entire middle school cheerleading squad was standing in the doorway.

"Oh, good. We found you!" said Cassidy.

For a second, I thought maybe they'd come to join our club, as a way of making it up to me for painting my face like a clown's, for humiliating me in front of Hunter. Cheerleaders cared about endangered animals, right? They could be warm-and-fuzzy people. I would know—I used to be one of them.

"You're late—" Olivia started to say.

"You're just in time," I said.

"Actually, Madison, could you come here for a second?" Cassidy asked in a slightly sweet, slightly syrupy, definitely superior tone.

"Why?" I asked. If she crossed the doorway, would

she automatically lose points with the eighth graders standing behind her?

"It's just that I have to tell you something and you're going to take it really, really hard." She paused.

What would she have to tell me? How many more things could go wrong today? "Go ahead," I said, walking over to her.

"Okay, but . . ." She shrugged. "You know that Halloween party I always have? At my house?" she asked.

I nodded. I'd been going to the Halloween parties at Cassidy's house since we were eight.

"Yeah, well, we decided to keep it really small this year. My mom doesn't want a lot of people so . . . sorry."

"She doesn't want a lot of people? Since when? Isn't that the point of your Halloween parties?" I asked.

"Not anymore. She wants me to be a little more, um, selective." She wrinkled her nose.

I didn't mind her changing the tradition, but not like this—not by being uninvited to something that I knew everyone else in our middle school would probably be at. "What are you saying? I'm uninvited?" I asked, just to make things clear.

She nodded.

"I'm uninvited," I said, repeating it so she'd hear how bad it sounded.

"I'm *really* sorry," she said with a pitying look at me.

I wanted to punch her a little bit when she did that. Me, the most nonviolent person on the planet. I'd never hurt an animal, endangered or not, but Cassidy? Was she on the protected list? After what she'd done to me today? "Yeah, I bet you are," I mumbled.

"What's that?"

"Oh, nothing." I smiled, putting on a brave face in front of the other cheerleaders.

"You understand. Right? I can't have everybody."

"No. Of course you can't." I looked at the floor, hoping to hide the tears that were stinging my eyes.

"Would you mind . . . you know. Breaking the news to Olivia and Taylor for me?" asked Cassidy.

"I can *hear* you," said Olivia. "I'm sitting right here."

Alexis glanced over at her. "Oh. We didn't notice."

Olivia stuck out her tongue.

"Don't sweat it," I said. "We weren't planning on coming. We made other plans that night, anyway." I forced myself to smile. We didn't have plans yet, but we could. For instance, trick or treating.

But inside all I could think was, what's the matter? I'm not cool enough for you now? How would I possibly ruin a party where there'd be a hundred guests? How did I matter that much?

Before they could say, or do, anything else, I took off down the hall.

"Madison? Madison!" Olivia called after me.

But I just kept running. I wanted to get far, far away from school.

Chapter 4

I bombed down the bumpy coastal road on my bike, wishing I could forget. I know it probably sounds dramatic, but I kept seeing this movie inside my head, sometimes running quickly, and sometimes in slow motion. But basically, the plot stayed the same. It showed a girl with green-streaked hair bumbling in front of a guy, then in front of a TV camera with a red face, then in the hallway.

All day, everyone at school had walked past me trilling their r's, or mentioning how it *was,* actually, the worst newscast they'd ever seen.

The rain in Maine falls mainly on Payneston, I thought as I headed into town. I rode along our small Main Street through a steady drizzle, my hooded rain jacket covering my helmet. The wind was blowing pretty strongly, too. I was halfway home, but I didn't want to go there.

Maybe it wasn't even raining in the rest of Payneston, I thought. Maybe it was only raining on my head, specifically.

The rain in Maine falls mainly on . . . me.

What would it be like if things were different? *How about if the rain in Maine fell mainly on the mean girls?*

I wished I had more options. I could go to Principal Monroe, and tell her that bullying was a serious problem at our school. But did what happened today qualify as bullying? Didn't bullying mean getting someone in a headlock and smashing them into a locker? Taking their money? Taunting them?

Besides, if I did something like talking to the principal, the mean girls would come after me in a way that would make today's troubles seem like nothing. Really, all I needed to do from now on was avoid Cassidy and the rest of my former friends. The school wasn't huge, but it was big enough that if I tried really, really hard . . .

Actually, it wasn't big enough. We shared classes. Our lockers were all down the same hall. I'd have to have plastic surgery so they would no longer recognize me. And that would make them tease me even more.

They'd had their little (okay, maybe not so little) laughs at my expense. Enough was enough. I couldn't take it anymore. But what could I possibly do?

That was when I saw the sign.

GRAND OPENING!

Just then the breeze picked up, and the rain started to fall even harder. As it did, I saw a little wooden sign swinging in the wind: COMBING ATTRACTIONS. It was designed like an old movie-house marquee, with colored bulbs all around it. I made a beeline toward it. It was a new hair salon, one I'd never seen before. A friendly sign in the window read NO APPOINTMENT NECESSARY.

First things first: I needed to get my hair fixed. I parked my bike under an awning, locked it, and headed for the salon. A red carpet led up the front steps.

I opened the door, and a small bell jingled. Inside, two stylists were taking care of a couple of clients: a woman was having her hair highlighted, and a man was getting a haircut. It looked like your standard beauty salon, but there was something offbeat about it, too.

Two gigantic combs were crossed above the shampoo sinks, and a mobile made from combs was hanging from the ceiling, directly above the counter. Old tin signs for beauty products covered the walls, along with framed print ads for a fancy brand of combs I'd never heard of. COMB ON OVER TO OUR SIDE and COMB AS YOU ARE signs welcomed clients to the waiting area, with comfy-looking chairs and a sofa, and a few coat hooks had been made from oversized combs. A beaded curtain made of colored empty nail polish bottles hung over a door with a sign that read PAINT-ON PLACE. Soft dance music played from the speakers.

"Hi there," one of the stylists said, as the man with the haircut left the salon. She looked like she was in her twenties. She had long, auburn-colored hair piled into a silver barrette, green eyes, and dark red, almost brown lipstick. She wore a black tank top, faded low-rise jeans, and a belt made from miniature license plates. She almost looked like she should have been in a rock band, not a hair salon. "How's the storm?"

"Not too bad," I said, looking around at all the products for sale, on glimmering silver shelves with pretty tinsel dangling off the tops, like trimmed silver hair. "At least it's not terrible yet, anyway."

"Give it time," she said. "How can I help you?"

I slid my umbrella into the holder by the front door, then set down my backpack and took off my bike helmet. "I was wondering. Do you sell Nik's Organix hair products?"

"I'm sorry, no," she replied.

"Really. Not at all? Not even the Original Sea Clean line?" I asked.

She shook her head. "I'm not familiar with those products."

"Really," I said. So this was one salon my mom hadn't gotten to yet. "Did you just move here or something?"

"No, I've been here for a while. I used to rent a chair at another place, though."

I opened my wallet to make sure I had enough money for a haircut and color. I'd saved the last couple of twenties I'd gotten for babysitting, and I had a Visa card as well. I hoped that would cover it.

"We kind of chose to go in a different direction with our products," the woman explained. "Will that be okay with you?"

I smiled. "Yeah. That's exactly what I want to do."

"Speaking of which—" She peered at my helmet hair. "Your color looks a bit different. I can't quite put my finger on it. Is that one of those at-home tint kits?"

34

"Not exactly. I need a new color, or a recolor," I said. "Please tell me you can fix this."

"Definitely I can fix it. Coloring can be wicked expensive," she replied. "But since you're a student, I'll cut you a deal."

"It's okay. I have a Visa gift card left from my birthday. Can I use that here?"

"Sure. I'll still give you a student rate, though."

"Thanks."

"I'm Poinsettia, by the way." She held out her hand for me to shake.

"What kind of a name is that?"

"Difficult for anyone to spell correctly." She reached into a drawer behind the desk, and handed me her business card, which I glanced at quickly. *Poinsettia R. Seasonal*, it said in loopy script, *Beauty Consultant.* "And what's your name?"

"Madison," I said. "Madison McCarrigan." Poinsettia didn't seem to recognize my last name. There wasn't that "McCarrigan? As in Nik McCarrigan? As in Nik's Organix?"

"My mom—" I started to say, but then I stopped. I didn't want Poinsettia to form an opinion of me based on my mom.

"What's that?"

"Oh, nothing," I said, waiting patiently while she swept up from her previous customer—who, judging from the amount of hair left on the floor, must have been a werewolf.

Poinsettia was wearing black boots and when she bent down to sweep up the clippings, I noticed they had high heels, little silver buckles on the sides, and pointed toes. They were the kind of boots I'd tried to convince my mom to buy for me once, when I went along on one of her business trips to Boston. I'd ended up with flat, furry kids' boots instead.

Poinsettia showed me a card with various hair color samples and we chose something close to my original color (whatever that was), but with a little extra shininess.

"What grade are you in?" Poinsettia asked as she draped a black cape over my shoulders.

I glanced up at her. "Seventh," I said.

"Really?"

I rolled my eyes. "I know, I know," I sighed. "You would have said younger."

"No, actually. Older. I don't get a lot of clients in here on their own at your age," she commented.

"Well, let's just say I'm really, really experienced at getting my hair trimmed, and cut, and washed."

"Huh." Poinsettia didn't seem to think that was strange . . . which *was* strange. "Well, you sit tight, I'll go grab the color and be right back," she said.

I looked around the salon while she was gone. There was the stylist working at a chair a little farther along who'd just finished giving a haircut. She was older, with short black hair streaked with purple. At least her streaks were cute—and intentional, I thought as the glare from the light broadcast my spinach-colored hair to the other customers.

When Poinsettia came back, the first thing she did was chop off the very ends of my hair. "No sense coloring split ends," she commented. Then she started painting the rest of my hair with a small brush.

"So I just don't know what I'm going to do," said the other stylist, who had the purple-streaked hair, edging closer to us. "He keeps calling and sending e-mails to apologize. It's like—he won't accept the fact that we're not dating anymore. But it's too late!"

"There's always a lot of drama around here," Poinsettia said to me. "You'd better get used to it because you're going to be here for a while."

"It's not drama! It's my life!" the other stylist said.

"See?" Poinsettia arched an eyebrow.

"That's okay," I said. "I'm used to drama." *You should have seen my day.*

"Okay, so what would *you* do?" the other stylist asked Poinsettia. "I want him to leave me alone. He broke my heart, now it's time for him to move on. I'm in a better place, or I'm trying to be, and I don't want him around me!"

"Well, here's what I would do," said Poinsettia as she applied the last touches of color to my hair with the brush. "I would write him a letter. And then I would burn it, and his name, in a glass jar. After that, you'll be free of him. You can move on with your life."

"And, um, why's that, exactly?" I asked, peeking out

from underneath my multiple hair clips. "I mean, why would that work?"

"Simple," she said. "You have to externally formalize everything you're informally internalizing. Know what I'm saying?"

I blinked a few times. Was it the fumes from the probably-not-organic hair color going to my head, or could something like this actually help us solve *our* problem? What if we could get rid of the mean girls that way? "That's kind of . . . out there. You really think that would work?" I asked.

"I'll try it," the other stylist said. "Can't hurt, right?"

I sat back, thinking furiously. I mean, my mom could go New Agey and hippie on me sometimes, but she'd never suggest anything like this. She'd just tell me to be nicer. I couldn't *be* any nicer, and the mean girls were still horrible to me. So maybe Poinsettia was onto something after all.

"Sometimes you have to take chances. You know?" Poinsettia asked.

I nodded as she set the timer for my hair color. "Oh, I know."

Chapter 5

My mother nearly fainted when I walked through the door at dinnertime. "Madison?" She grabbed the kitchen island to steady herself. "What did you do?"

I was the one who should have been shocked. She was cooking dinner on a Monday night. My mom, the queen of ordering in, who never met a takeout menu she didn't like.

That's not totally fair, I guess. She used to cook a lot, but ever since her company got successful and took off, she hardly ever has the time on weekdays. Mom started out as a crunchy granola hippie, then went corporate. She's still vegetarian—technically a pescetarian, which means she eats fish, too—but most of the time we either go out for dinner or order takeout.

Some people think Mom and I look alike, because we both have strawberry-blond hair and green eyes. We're about the same height, and apparently have the same eyebrows, which is a weird attribute to share, if you ask me. You'd think DNA would have more important things to do than go around determining eyebrow shapes.

At the moment, we didn't look that much alike anymore. She still had her long, straight hair, and I now had a short bob that stopped just below my chin line. I was still wearing my T-shirt, jeans, and corduroy jacket, and Mom had on one of her flowing hemp outfits. (Even when she wore a business suit, she had on an unbleached cotton camisole underneath.)

"Kind of obvious what I did, huh? So, what do you think?" I asked.

"Uh, I guess the important thing is what do *you* think?" she asked.

"I like it." I gazed at my reflection in our stainless steel toaster. "It's different."

"Different. Yes." She reached out to touch the back of my head, where my hair now stopped. "Are we feeling all right?"

"I am. I don't know about you," I said, backing away. She had this glazed, confused expression that made me think dinner wasn't going to turn out well. The brown rice would be burned, veggies scorched, and tofu done to the point of crumbling into sawdust.

"Oh, wow. Did you color it, too? You colored it!" she suddenly cried.

"Mom, I had to," I said. "It was green this morning, thanks to your baby shampoo experiments last night."

"What kind of color did you get? Where?" A look of horror crossed her face. "It wasn't *chemical*, was it?"

She was acting like I'd suddenly started doing drugs.

Then suddenly her eyes brightened. "No, you know what, this is great, this is fantastic. I've been trying to develop this line of stuff just for shorter hair, called Original *Short* Clean, and it's all about special extra-light shampoos for—"

"No, Mom. I've had enough." The words were out before I even had time to think about them. I realized this was something I'd wanted to say to my mother for a long time now.

"Enough?" she asked.

"Of me having to be your girl guinea pig for all your hair products. That's half the reason I wanted to cut my hair," I said.

"It is?" She looked genuinely stunned, and I guess I couldn't blame her. I'd never really been honest with her about this before.

"Yes, Mom. I mean, what's wrong with using Parker for a change? Or David, or—"

"Their hair is not receptive to formulas designed mainly for longer hair—and, well, David hardly *has* any hair, for one thing."

"Aha! You tried out your stuff on him too many times, didn't you? *That's* why he's bald," I teased her. My mom's boyfriend shaved his head, which often looked like a shiny bowling ball. To me, it was kind of ironic that the organic hair care product queen of Maine was dating someone with absolutely *no* hair.

"You said that I was half the reason for this drastic change," Mom said. "What's the other reason?"

41

I shrugged, not sure how much I wanted to explain. "I didn't exactly have what we call a stellar day."

"No?" She looked genuinely concerned, but I wasn't sure if it was about me, or the veggies that were about to burn. She quickly turned it off.

I saw the video of me on TV in my brain again. "No."

"Want to talk about it?" she prompted.

"Mmm . . ." I shook my head. "Definitely not."

"I'm worried. You've had long hair since . . . since . . ." She started to sniffle a little bit.

"Since forever. I know."

"Since you were born," she sniffled.

"I don't think I was born with long hair," I said. "Unless you adopted me from a monkey house." She still looked sad, so I added, "Mom, you know how it is when something just has to change. And you don't know what it is, so you try . . . anything."

Mom looked at me as if she was finally getting it. "But, honey . . . why didn't you just ask me to stop?"

"I did ask," I said.

"Oh. Yes, I guess you did. But didn't we have fun—I mean, can't we still have fun?"

"Honestly, it was fun, a lot of the time. And I'm glad to help out, and when you featured me on your website, that was really cool," I admitted. "But lately—the thing is, Mom? I can't afford to have bad hair days. Ever again."

"What? Why not? Did something happen?"

42

"That's kind of an understatement. Someone made fun of my hair this morning. Someone . . . kind of . . . cute. And boylike." Not that I considered Hunter as any sort of potential boyfriend or anything, especially not after today, but he did still count as a boy. Sometimes what they—the boy species—thought counted.

"I'm sorry," she said.

I briefly considered telling her everything: the mean trick with Hunter, the altered news text, the clown face Cassidy had painted on me, the chocolate bras.

"But maybe he was just trying to be funny. I mean, was it really that bad?" Mom reached out and touched my shorter hair.

"When I went to get it cut today, the stylist said it looked like peas. Which is funny because Hunter Matthews said it looked like seaweed. Which isn't as bad as Alexis calling it overcooked spinach."

"Ew. Well, what do they know? Green is the new black." She laughed.

I glared at her. "Not funny. My hair used to be strawberry blond, remember? Not veggie-green. That edamame concept you had? Not good."

"Sorry about that. But why didn't you let me cut it?" she asked. "I've always cut your hair."

"I know, but the thing is, Mom? I needed it colored, too. I needed everything to be fixed as soon as possible. And . . . look. I need to be a little less . . . experimented on in the future."

"Oh." She put her hand to her throat, which was

covered with a pashmina. She nodded. "Okay. I get it, I think."

"Thanks." I headed upstairs to my room.

"Dinner will be ready in fifteen minutes!" she called up the stairs after me.

I'd have to see it to believe it. I dumped my backpack onto my desk, and sat down to snuggle with Rudy for a minute, like I did whenever I got home from school. My cat loves to sleep in my bed when I'm gone—sometimes even under the covers.

We live on this tiny peninsula jutting out into the ocean. My bedroom has a long, rectangular window that I love to look out of while I lie on my bed writing or talking on the phone. I watch lobster boats, seagulls, sailboats—sometimes even just the clouds. That afternoon the storm was providing lots to admire: crashing surf and water spraying into the wind. I loved it when the sea was dramatic.

I jumped up and checked my reflection in the mirror above my dresser. The new haircut still looked good. Maybe I'd get sick of looking at it soon, but not yet. I wondered what everyone at school would think when I showed up the next day.

Did I kind of look more like Gianni, my biological (and so far, only) dad now? Stylish, sort of?

On my dresser I had a framed photo of me, Mom, and Gianni. I didn't see him very often, and I didn't know if it was his fault, my fault, or my mom's fault. Sometimes I wondered why my mom wanted to do this parenting thing on her own. Sometimes I wish there was another parent around because my mom's advice isn't always that helpful.

Gianni had been a good friend of my mom's at the Fashion Institute of Technology in New York, where she went to college, living outside of Maine for about ten years. Mom and Gianni both ended up leaving FIT and going into the "hair couture" field instead. Gianni thought it might be a good match for my mom, but *he* wouldn't be a good match for my mom because he had a boyfriend.

Oops.

She was crushed, or so she says, but they worked it out to become best pals. When she wanted kids but didn't want to get married (she's the kind of person who really gets a kick out of doing unusual things, which annoys my grandparents to no end), she decided he was the perfect guy to have them with.

Sometimes I don't know why she tells me this stuff, because it's really *personal*. You know?

She named me Madison after Madison Avenue, which I guess is a big destination, fashion-wise. My little brother, Parker? He was also created in a test tube (sorry—TMI), but he wasn't named after a New York street. He was named after our Grandpa McCarrigan, which made my grandparents a lot more accepting of Mom's whole single-parent test-tube-babies plan.

I think when my mom moved back to Maine and

started her own business as the shampoo hippie, before she morphed into this corporate, wealthy CEO type who still dressed like a hippie, she was, basically, a flake. Her flakiness still comes through in her creative product ideas, but now she actually gets paid a lot for being flaky. (But not having flakes, à la dandruff. That could be a career killer.)

Sometimes I think that Olivia must be Mom's daughter, not me. They can both be so clueless. They should have passports from la-la land.

Anyway, Gianni's more like a distant cousin than anything. He sends lots of stuff to me from his work at fashion shows both abroad and in New York, where he's a hair stylist for a couple of runway supermodels. Sometimes I have some of the coolest clothes at school—especially T-shirts with unique colors, cuts, or logos.

Not that anyone there recognizes this, or cares. They're too busy all wearing the same stuff from Abercrombie, L.L.Bean, or Aèropostale.

The cool thing about being best friends with Cassidy years ago was that she had only her mom, too, so the two of us were in day care together because our moms worked full-time, and nothing seemed off at the time about them being single moms. (Cassidy's dad had moved about an hour away and she saw him every other weekend.) My mom would always say that "lots of people have different family situations and there's nothing wrong with that."

Now Cassidy's mom was remarried so she had a stepfather, and my mom had her on-again, off-again thing with David. He wasn't part of our family, and he wasn't *not* part of it, if that makes any sense.

Cassidy and I used to be good friends. We attended the same preschool, where we both liked to wear dresses and spin a lot—according to Mom, anyway. I've blocked it out. Then, as we got older, we took dance classes together.

I had an empty fish tank on my big desk, under my loft bed. I used to have fish, but when we moved into this house a few years ago, I started to feel really guilty. Here I was, living right on the water . . . on the ocean . . . and then having these captive fish. I wanted to free them but I knew they wouldn't survive in the cold Atlantic water, but still, it seemed wrong that they had to *look* at it.

So when they went to the great fish tank in the sky, I gave them a proper burial at sea and didn't replace them. Instead, I cleaned out the tank and turned it into a display case for my old dolls and their fashionable outfits. So it's my doll tank now. They look sort of bizarre, but it's like a department store window that I keep designing.

Looking at my dolls, I thought about how once last year Cassidy and I had taken my Malibu Barbie and turned her into Bar Harbor Barbie for a school project—we'd made orange rubber boots for her, and built a lobster trap from toothpicks. (They tend not to make dolls and toys about Maine because we're not as glamorous as California—but if you want a red stuffed lobster, there are a hundred to choose from.)

But sometime last year things changed with Cassidy. It had started out with small things I didn't really notice at the time. Like one time she uninvited me to a sleepover at her house, telling me at the last second that it was called off. Then I found out at school that it hadn't been—she'd just decided to invite Alexis instead.

Or the time we had plans to go to the movies, and she didn't show up. I finally called her, and she said, "Oh, something came up."

It was agonizing at first. I used to lie awake at night and wonder: why did she want to be friends with them, instead of me? Why couldn't we all be friends, like we used to be?

There was this weird, almost geological shift happening, like Cassidy and I were two glaciers moving in opposite directions.

"What happened? You used to be such good friends," my mom walked around saying, for what seemed like weeks on end.

"Mom, things change. People change," I'd try to explain.

"Not *that* much."

"Yes, they do. You don't understand!"

"Just call her," my mom would say over and over.

"It's a misunderstanding, that's all. You don't stop being friends overnight."

The first couple of times I took Mom's advice and called Cassidy, the only person at her house who wanted to talk to me was her *mom*. She'd go on about how much she missed me, and ask why I hadn't been to their house lately, but I didn't want to say, "Because your daughter is being kind of a jerk to me lately."

At the same time, my mom was stuck a decade back, wondering why Cassidy and I didn't wear the same dresses or take ballet anymore.

Meanwhile, the same thing was happening with Team Tay-Kay, when Kayley decided she wouldn't do any extra training sessions with Taylor anymore because it "ruined her concentration." And Olivia and Alexis stopped co-owning the bunny they'd shared for two years because Alexis suddenly decided keeping bunnies as pets was way too juvenile for her.

Maybe those things wouldn't have been terrible on their own. People grow apart and all that. But Kayley, Cassidy, and Alexis couldn't seem to let well enough alone. They had to openly drop us. Repeatedly. In public. They quit riding bikes to school with us, turned the other way when we passed them in the halls, and, worst of all, blocked the chairs around their lunch table when we tried to sit with them the second day of seventh grade. By the time we quit arguing with them about it, we were left with no place to sit, and carried our lunches to a couple of folding chairs in the corner, by the racks where everyone left their dirty dishes and used trays.

It was beyond embarrassing.

So, maybe Poinsettia was right.

Time for big changes.

Changes were good.

I heard a noise like something snorting—a small whale, maybe. I turned from the mirror, and there was Parker, standing in the doorway. "What are you doing in here?" I asked. "You're supposed to knock fir—"

"Whoa," he said, stepping back. "I didn't know the storm was *that* bad."

"What do you mean? The surf?" I asked, looking over my shoulder at the whitecaps in the ocean.

"No. I mean, it blew your hair away," he said, laughing.

"Get out. Out!" I ran over and slammed the door behind him.

Little brothers should not be seen or heard.

Maybe I should work on a plan to get *him* out of my life, too, I thought. As soon as possible.

Chapter 6

"Where did you *get* that adorable cut?" Olivia cried when I walked into the Whale after supper and pulled my umbrella out of the twisting wind. I'd called my friends and asked them to meet me at Olivia's parents' restaurant as soon as they were done eating.

"A new place, on Main Street. Combing Attractions," I said.

"It's really cute!" Olivia ran over to take my raincoat and hang it on the rack just inside the door. "I love it, Madison." She was already a lot better at talking with her braces.

Olivia was wearing sparkling silver long-bead earrings. She made all her own jewelry with bead kits, and was always giving us new homemade bracelets and necklaces for presents. I hoped her dangling metal earrings didn't get caught in her new metal braces. I didn't know why I thought that, but I did.

"Never heard of it," said Taylor. She wore a green Payneston High hoodie, jeans, and blue plaid rain boots that squeaked as she swiveled on the stool. "The color is awesome! So did your mom fix that for you?"

"I got it fixed myself, actually. At the salon," I said.

"Why didn't you tell us you were going to get your hair cut?" asked Taylor. "We totally would have gone with you."

"Yeah, you ran out on me. I didn't know where you went," said Olivia.

"I don't know." I walked over to the counter and slid onto a stool next to Taylor. "It was a spur-of-the-moment decision. I didn't know I was going to do it until I did it." I waved hello to Olivia's mom, who was at the host stand, while her dad was probably somewhere back in the kitchen. They made the best fish chowder for miles around—not to mention their fried clams—but they served seafood lots of different ways, too.

"Do you remember when Kayley dyed her hair purple, so then I dyed *my* hair because we were Team Tay-Kay, only mine didn't come out right and I had that magenta streak straight down the middle like I was a really weird skunk?" Taylor said. "My dad went absolutely ballistic, 'You have a meet coming up and nobody goes into a meet looking like that, what were you thinking?' and we had to go to the drugstore and stay up like half the night dying it back to brown, except it was more like black?"

"How could I forget that?" said Olivia. "I think we went through about eight towels that day. So, if your mom wasn't there when you got your hair colored, what did she say when she saw it?"

"She's trying to deal with it." On my way out that night, she'd actually admitted that it was not a horrible thing.

"So. What's your idea?" Olivia asked. We all scooted in close to the counter.

I looked over my shoulder at the restaurant to make sure nobody we knew happened to be in hearing range. I caught Cameron Hansen's eye—he was there with his family—and waved awkwardly. *Hi, remember me? The idiot from this morning's update with the red face and the green hair? Yeah, it's the new and improved me, now.*

I hope.

"Well, I was thinking we need to kind of clean the slate, you know, with Cassidy and everyone," I said.

"Clean the slate? How?" asked Taylor, squinting at me.

"When Cassidy and I were friends, we said we'd always, always have our hair long," I explained. "We had to have the same headbands, the same braids, everything. I just don't want anything in common with her anymore. I want to cut all our connections."

"So, you're done!" Olivia gave me a high five. "Hair cut, mission accomplished."

"Not exactly," I said. "I mean, it's only a start."

"Um . . . what do you mean?" asked Olivia. "Are you planning to cut it even shorter?"

I laughed. "No—I just meant it's the start of something."

"You're losing me," she said. "Have a fry."

53

"What are you thinking?" Taylor asked me. "You sound like you have a plan."

I shook my head and felt the strange sensation of my short hair moving on my neck. "Here's the thing. While I was having my hair cut, this other stylist kept talking about breaking up with this guy, and my stylist said she should write him a letter and then burn it. She said it would help her get him out of her life. He'd leave her alone after that," I explained.

"Burn his name? And a letter?" Olivia shook her head. "Sounds crazy. Who is this person, anyway?"

"I don't know. She was coloring my hair at the time. I might have missed some of the details," I admitted with a smile. "But just think about it for a sec," I urged. "We want the mean girls out of our lives, right? We want them to stop harassing us. So why not give the same thing a try?"

"Sure," said Olivia, spraying me a little. "Something *like* that, maybe. But . . . that?"

"I just wish I could completely ignore them," I said. "I hate that it matters to me what they think or do, when they obviously don't care about us."

"I know, it's not logical," Taylor added. "I keep trying not to care if Kayley does better than me this year or whether she goes to state or whatever." She sighed. "But I do. So then I tell my mom, and she's like, well, you just have to be teammates, you don't have to be friends, that's part of growing up, blah blah blah." She paused. "So what were you saying, Madison?"

I drained the last of my soda and pushed the glass away. "I want us to have a good-bye party for them."

"A party with them?" Olivia asked. "Are you nuts?"

"She didn't say *with* them," Taylor pointed out. "She said *for* them. As in, good-bye. To get them out of our lives. Right?" She looked at me, and I nodded.

"Well . . . how?" asked Olivia.

"That's the part I don't know yet," I said. "I was hoping we could use your computer and look up some ideas. I mean, I know we can have the party at my house. We have a fireplace and we can definitely burn their names. But what else?"

"Let's see." Olivia had her computer on the counter, where she often sat to do her homework while her parents worked. She looked over at the two of us. "What are we talking here? A witch thing? Witch dot com?"

"No, no." I shook my head. "Something more civilized."

"Definitely," said Taylor. "I am not into potions and spells."

"Me neither. I couldn't even read the first Harry Potter," said Olivia.

While we were talking, Olivia found some articles on self-help sites about how to deal with negative energy and get rid of "toxic" people. We weren't really sure if that's what we meant.

"Let's plan on the name-in-flames stuff," Taylor said. "But what else can we do for a good-bye party?"

I pictured tossing Bar Harbor Barbie into the fire. Probably that would create an environmental disaster. So maybe we wouldn't burn everything—maybe we'd burn the names, but just put away a box of things from the time when we were BFFs.

"Whatever we do, it will have to involve lots of snacks and a movie," said Olivia.

"Why?" I asked.

"Because all our fun nights do," she said. "Duh." She reached for a small bowl of mixed nuts on the counter and took a handful.

"Then we'll eat anti-mean snacks," I said.

Olivia's forehead creased in thought. "What are anti-mean snacks?"

"I don't know. Sweet things? Anything with lots of sugar?" I guessed. "Do I have to come up with everything?"

"How about 'mean-free,'" Olivia suggested. "You know, in the tradition of sugar-free, gluten-free . . ."

"Sounds good," said Taylor.

"What night should we have the party?" I asked. "Saturday?"

"I can't Saturday," both Olivia and Taylor said at the same time.

"Okay . . . how about Friday?"

"Well, what are the chances we'll go to the dance Friday?" asked Olivia.

"Uh, slim," I said. I thought about Hunter and how Cassidy had pushed me to talk to him about the dance, when all he wanted was my homework so he could go to the dance. With someone else. *Her,* probably.

"What's so special about it, anyway," commented Taylor. "I bet it will be totally boring."

Suddenly Olivia turned to us with a deadly serious expression. She looked pained, like she had just bitten her cheeks with her braces.

"What?" I asked. "What's wrong?"

She adjusted one of her earrings, which had gotten tangled in her hair. "You know that old saying, don't shoot the messenger?"

Taylor and I both nodded.

"Madison, I really don't want to show you this. But I have to," Olivia said. "I was looking for stuff about the eighth-grade dance, just in case, you know, we wanted to know more . . . and I came across this. It's like . . . evil."

She turned the computer toward us, and I saw in big letters: PAYNESTON PEEPS. That's our school's social networking site.

And right below that, under Today's Update (still not favorite words of mine):

GOING ATTRACTIONS

WHAT SEVENTH GRADER RECENTLY LOPPED OFF HER MARTIAN-GREEN LOCKS? WE THINK SHE LOST HER BEST FEATURE, BUT YOU BE THE JUDGE.

VOTE ON "BEFORE" AND "AFTER"!

View results here.

"Before" was the picture Alexis had taken of me

outside school that morning. Hunter was standing behind me, holding up his fingers in a V above my head.

I really did hate him now.

Wow. It really was that *green,* I thought.

Under "after," there was a picture of me walking out of Combing Attractions that afternoon. My hair was blowing all over the place in the wind, and some strands seemed to be floating straight up to the sky. I looked slightly possessed, or like I'd been caught in an electrical storm.

Funny. I didn't remember seeing anyone on Main Street when I left, but maybe I was too excited about the new look and how I felt, like I'd left some of my problems—seaweed spinach hair—on the salon floor. Apparently not.

"Do you, um, want to see the results?" asked Olivia.

"No." Hot tears stung my eyes. I couldn't believe they'd gone this far. Mocking me online for *everyone* to see?

If I'd had any doubts about our plan to get them out of our lives, they were gone.

"So." Taylor put her arm around my shoulder. "Friday night sound okay?"

Chapter 7

The next four days went by quickly.

I kept a low profile at school. Extremely low. Even if I did look better, I certainly didn't feel any better—especially not whenever I thought about being uninvited to Cassidy's Halloween party, or the "before and after" blog comments she, Alexis, and Kayley had made. I just knew they had to be behind the Peeps post. Who else would do something like that? Olivia told me it had been taken down, but it was too late.

Who needed their stupid party, anyway? We had our own to plan.

Friday night, I walked into the kitchen to find Parker glued to the computer, playing a video game.

This wouldn't do. I had a dozen things I wanted to accomplish before the others showed up at seven, and even though I'd had all week to get ready? I was still not ready.

Gianni always said that creative people made the best procrastinators. Or maybe it was the other way around.

Anyway, my friends were on their way to our house,

and I was feeling unprepared. Did that mean I was especially creative, or especially lazy?

Never mind. I had to make Rice Krispies Treats. Not that it's a complicated recipe, but you know—even a not-so-top chef needs to concentrate.

"Could you leave?" I asked Parker, for what seemed like the ninth time, but was probably only the fifth. "Could you just sort of disappear tonight? This is really important."

"Oh, yeah. Crucial," Parker said. He didn't look up or tear himself away from Illegal Death Ride VII. He tapped at the keys as I poured snapping, crackling, popping cereal (hey, it says so on the box) into a pan of melted marshmallows. "It's a sleepover. Since when is a sleepover vitally important?"

"Since when do you know what the word *vitally* means?" I replied.

"I'm younger than you. I'm not *dumber* than you," he said. He scooted closer to the table and fired off some key explosions that made the riders careen into oblivion. "Yes!"

I didn't expect him to understand, much less be sympathetic. I think he used to have a sort of little-brother crush on Cassidy and he hadn't forgiven me for not being friends with her anymore. He'd always acted a little extra goofy when she was around.

"Since this sleepover is . . . look, it's hard to explain," I said. "You wouldn't understand."

"Oh, right, because I don't understand . . . eating

munchies, watching movies, and sleeping in sleeping bags." He swiped some gooey marshmallow that was left in the saucepan. "Is Cassidy coming?"

"No," I said. "Definitely not."

"Then why are you making Rice Krispies Treats with chocolate chips?"

"Because they're Cassidy's favorite snack."

"Okay . . . have you lost your mind? Are you even listening to yourself?" asked Parker. "You just said Cassidy's not coming. You're not really hanging out with Cassidy anymore."

I sighed. "I *know*. I *realize* that."

"So . . . why are you making her favorite snack?"

"Because—look. This party tonight, it's because . . . we're trying to get Cassidy and her friends, who used to be our friends, to quit harassing us and just leave us alone," I explained. "Because we're not friends anymore, and they're not exactly nice to us."

"Seriously? Cassidy's not nice?"

"Yup."

"Why not?" asked Parker.

"Ask her," I suggested.

"Maybe I will."

"No, you won't," I said. "Please don't talk to her."

"Make up your mind. And what does making her favorite Rice Krispies Treats have to do with not talking to her anymore?" he asked.

"We're . . . going to sort of smash them," I said. "Or eat them. Or throw them in the fire or something."

"You're getting really weird as you get older." Parker looked at me as if I'd lost my mind, and actually, I did think I was starting to sound that way. "That's a waste. Give them to me instead," he said. "I'll eat half, then take the other half to Cassidy's house and tell her you're sorry. Or, instead of burning dessert, why don't you just tell them to leave you alone?"

Sometimes Parker is kind of right about things, and insightful, which kind of makes me hate him. Maybe he was right this time, that the bigger and stronger thing to do would have been to confront them and just say, "Leave me alone and don't write hurtful posts about my hair."

But that wasn't dramatic, and it wouldn't change anything, either. And the fact that an immature ten-year-old could point out that this whole idea was sort of, well, immature, made me sad.

"But I'm *not* sorry!" I cried. "She's the one who should be sorry." Fortunately my mother came into the kitchen just then. "Mom, make Parker leave," I insisted.

She laughed. "What do you think I am, a witch?"

I froze, mid-stir of the sticky marshmallow mix. If my mother were a witch, would she be able to help me with tonight's ceremony? "Uh, why did you say that?" I asked.

"Because, I don't have supernatural powers to get Parker to leave," she said. "I suppose I could ask him nicely, or you could ask him more nicely than you just did."

Was this really a time to go all Emily Post on me?

"Parker," I said with a phony smile. "Would you mind not being here when my friends show up? And could you please stay invisible throughout the entire night? Because if you do that, I might promise I will save some good food for you."

"Define 'some,'" he said.

"Lots."

"Okay," he agreed. "I will gladly get lost. It's not like I *want* to be here."

"And it's not like I want you to be here, either."

"We're on our way upstairs, Madison," said Mom. "We'll check back in a while."

"No, don't," I muttered.

Mom coughed. "We will check back in a while," she repeated slowly, giving me The Look. She sounded as if she was gritting her teeth a bit, too. What was *she* so stressed about? I was the one trying to change my life with one measly sleepover. She ought to meditate for a while and just chill out.

"Right. That'd be great. See you soon!" I hoped she understood I was under a lot of pressure: hosting, baking, and plotting the demise of former friendships.

I pressed the marshmallow and cereal into a rectangular cake pan. I'd never cooked something before that I planned on trashing. It did seem pretty wasteful. Maybe we should rethink this part of the plan, I decided.

No sooner had I finished the Rice Krispies Treats

and washed my hands than there was a knock at the back door.

Taylor walked in first, and then Olivia. Each carried a backpack, a sleeping bag, and some kind of food.

"Yay, you're here! What did you guys bring?" I asked.

"I made devil's food cake." Taylor set a domed cake plate on the counter. "Three layers. My grandmother's special recipe. Okay, technically my mom and I made it together—actually she made the cake part and I did the frosting. Some of the frosting."

"Sounds delish, but I don't get it," I said.

"It's *devil's* food cake," Taylor said again. "You know, in honor of our former friends. Or enemies. Sometimes it's hard to know what category to put them in."

"Devils? Isn't that kind of harsh? They're not devils," I said.

"Well, they're certainly not angels," Olivia said. "We must have been on the same wavelength. I brought deviled eggs."

Taylor held her nose as Olivia pried open the red Ziploc container. "I hate deviled eggs."

"Really? I love them." I leaned in to pick one up.

Taylor spoke in a nasal tone, still holding her nose. "They smell funny. Plus, they have weird orange powder sprinkled on top."

"Paprika." I swallowed the deviled egg and looked around the kitchen sheepishly. Olivia and Taylor were staring at me. "What? Are we not eating yet?" I asked.

"If you're so worried, don't have any," Olivia said to Taylor. "We'll save them all for Madison." She snapped the cover back on and slid the container to me. I put them into the fridge.

Taylor reached into her canvas tote bag and took out a large jar. "I also brought dill pickles. I was thinking that what we do tonight will get us out of a pickle."

Olivia licked a gob of marshmallow off her thumb. "I eat pickles like five times a week. It hasn't helped."

"Yes, but that was before you were trying to focus," Taylor said in a very serious voice.

Olivia started laughing. "You sound crazy."

"Oh, and you don't?" Taylor teased back.

"Pickles, deviled eggs, and marshmallows. We're going to get so sick. Aren't we?" I asked, laughing. "I made Cassidy's favorite snack. So, we've got all the bases covered. We can eat their favorite foods and really rich food with a devilish aspect to it. Or we can just, like, eat nothing and not get sick. Come on, let's get started."

"Eating?" asked Olivia.

"Meeting. Let's get what we need. The sun's going down," I said.

"Do your powers run out at dark or something?" Taylor teased. "We have all night, right?"

"So what do we do first?" asked Olivia.

"First, let's go in the living room. I have a box there—did you guys bring things to put in storage?" We'd planned to take something important from each of us that represented that time in our lives when we were pals with the mean girls, and put everything into a box, to cut those connections, too. We wouldn't burn them, though, just in case there was a time when we got nostalgic and wanted to have them back. Somehow I didn't think that would happen, but you never knew. Besides, I was sure some of the things in the box would stink up the house if we tried to burn them.

Taylor took off her Shawn Johnson pendant. "Kayley and I bought matching ones after the Beijing Olympics. I still love Shawn Johnson, but . . ." She placed the pendant in the box.

"Olivia, you're next," I said.

"This is good. Really, really good." Olivia reached into her brown shopping bag and pulled out a towel. She unwrapped the towel, and lifted out a brightly colored ceramic plate. "For Alexis's tenth birthday party, we made plates at Paint Your Plate. Look at all the little messages we put on there. And I drew a picture of her dog. Of course, now her *dog* won't even talk to me." We started laughing, but as Olivia handed the plate over to me to put into the box, it slipped from her hand.

The plate fell onto the tile floor surrounding the fireplace and smashed into a dozen pieces. "Oh, no— I'm so sorry!" I said.

"It's not your fault—I'm the one who dropped it." Olivia leaned down to pick up the pieces; there were three large pieces, and several small ones.

"I think that's bad luck," Taylor said. "Seven years?

We'll be in college by the time it wears off."

"No, that's mirrors. Besides, I wasn't going to be using the plate anymore, right?" Olivia laughed as she put the three big pieces of the plate into the box. I grabbed the small broom we kept by the fireplace for cleaning up ash, and swept up the small shards.

"Okay, Madison, it's your turn," Taylor said.

"I have these." I held up a set of pom-poms from when Cassidy and I did cheer together in sixth grade.

"And these." I put an old pair of pink ballet slippers in the box.

"And this." I held up a program from a dance recital we'd done when we were six.

"Oh, I can't forget this." I showed them a small silver bracelet—Cassidy and I had worn matching ones at about the same time we wore identical clothes. Which was most of elementary school.

"Not to mention these." I pointed to a stack of books on the footstool. "We used to trade books back and forth all the time."

"I think you're going to have to narrow it down. The box isn't that big," Olivia said.

"Okay. I'll pick what seems most important." I slid the ballet slippers in with the dance program, two paperbacks, and one pom-pom. "Done. Can one of you seal it up while I start the fire? And can the other one write down the names so we can toss them in when the fire is ready?"

Olivia picked up the roll of packing tape and pulled

off a strip. "What should I write on here?" She grabbed a bottle of nail polish from the collection I'd put on the coffee table for our sleepover. We usually paint our toenails while we sit around watching movies. "How about, 'our stuff'?"

A minute later, while I was stacking logs in the fireplace, I heard Olivia say, "Why isn't this showing . . . ? Oh, hold on a second. I grabbed clear." She started laughing.

"Here, Oblivia, use this." Taylor handed her a bottle of purple glitter polish. "I'm done." She waved the sheet of paper in the air, showing us Cassidy's, Kayley's, and Alexis's names written in large letters.

"I just want to get this over with," Olivia said. "It's starting to feel kind of creepy. Like voodoo dolls. Then again, those don't work. *This* is going to work. Right?"

"Wait a second. When did you try voodoo dolls?" Taylor asked.

"Remember that time your neck hurt really badly, and you thought it was from a new trick you did on the balance beam?" Olivia asked.

Taylor's eyes widened. "Seriously?"

Olivia giggled. "No, I'm only joking. Why would I do that to you?" She laughed again. "I actually tried it on someone else."

"Who?"

"I refuse to answer on the grounds it might incriminalize me," said Olivia.

"Incriminate," I corrected her.

"Whatever. I'm not saying." Olivia smiled. "So, how's that fire coming along?" She nudged me in the side.

I backed away from the fireplace. I'd arranged the logs and stuffed kindling underneath them, and now all I had to do was throw in a lit match. Easy, right? I lit a match. And then another and another. Each one went out instantly as soon as I laid it in the fireplace.

I grabbed some sheets of newspaper from the bin beside the fireplace and stuffed them under the kindling. I lit the newspaper on fire with a new match, then turned around. "Ready?"

Olivia waved the paper with the mean girls' names on it in the air. "Ready." She tossed it in the fireplace. We all stood back, waiting for the paper to catch fire. But the newspaper hadn't ignited the kindling, which didn't ignite the logs. The names just sat there, turning slightly tan, smoldering on a log.

Why was this taking so long? I glanced at the clock above the fireplace. It was already seven fifty-five, and we wanted to watch a movie that started at eight.

"Light already!" I cried. I looked around for something else to put in to make the fire happen. I grabbed the extra black and green pom-pom and tossed it in.

WHOOSH! There was an instant, blazing fire.

Taylor clapped her hand over her face, covering her nose. "Ew! That stinks. Why is there so much smoke?"

"Uh-oh. I think we just polluted the entire house," Olivia said.

Mom came running down the stairs, fanning the air.

"What happened? Is everything okay? What smells so badly?"

I shrugged, trying to look innocent. "I made a fire?"

She fiddled with something inside the fireplace. "You forgot to open the flue. How many times do I have to remind you about the flue? Then again, how often do you try to start fires on your own?" She glanced over her shoulder at me. "What's the occasion?"

"Um, nothing. Just thought it'd be cozy," I said.

She opened a couple of windows in the living room and a strong fall breeze rushed into the room. So much for cozy, but at least we weren't getting poisoned by burning plastic. Mom peered into the fireplace again. "What's *in* there, anyway?"

I couldn't tell her that it was a pom-pom. She'd call the Environmental Protection Agency to report me. "Oh, just some, um, shredded paper I was using to get it started," I said. "From the, um, paper shredder." Fortunately it looked as if the paper with the mean girls' names had already been incinerated.

"That was very smart of you, recycling something that's already been used. Thinking of the environment. I like that. Nice job, Madison." She smiled and then headed back upstairs.

Nice job? That was a close one, I thought as I collapsed on the sofa. If my eco-mom found out we were tossing pom-poms into the fireplace, she'd probably send me to jail herself. "Well, that's that. I guess we can put the mean girls out of our minds for a while. Does anyone else feel funny? Sort of different?" I asked.

Olivia laughed. "Why would I feel different?"

"I don't know." I rubbed my arms. "I just got the shivers."

"That's because your mom opened the windows. Remember? Let's close them and get some snacks before the movie starts!" said Taylor.

"And then let's paint our nails," said Olivia.

"Okay. First, I'm going to put this away, somewhere safe. I'll be right back." I picked up our time capsule box and brought it out to the garage, where we have tons of storage space. I set it on a shelf up high, above the boxes of surplus hair products. Then I grabbed some of our snacks and went back into the living room.

"You always hog the sofa, Olivia. A little *room*, please?" Taylor was saying, pushing at Olivia's legs.

"What? I do not," said Olivia, pushing back.

"Move over," Taylor urged, pushing Olivia.

"Hey." Olivia glared at her.

"Great, guys." I sighed. "While you were arguing, we missed the opening. Everyone knows the opening scene is the best one in the whole movie."

"If you hadn't taken so long to start the fire, maybe we wouldn't have missed it," Taylor said.

"Come on, guys. Lighten up!" said Olivia. "We're just supposed to be having fun, kicking back."

"You're right, you're right," I said. "Pass the pickles."

We started laughing, and suddenly, everything was just fine between us. Better, even. We'd removed the mean girls from our lives. What could be better?

Chapter 8

I didn't do much over the rest of the weekend. I spent a lot of time designing our Endangered Animals Club T-shirts; maybe nobody would join, but if we could sell shirts to the rest of the school, we could still raise money for the cause.

Mom had put up the money for a hundred blank tees, and we'd gotten iron-on designs and some fabric paint at the fabric store. While Taylor was at a meet in Portland, Olivia and I spent all of Saturday afternoon designing, painting, and ironing. Each shirt would be unique, a one of a kind creation. A collectible, really.

They wouldn't be pictures of animals. Middle schoolers were way too old to go for that. Instead they were colors, random words, and patterns. They were very artistic, if I do say so myself.

By the end of the afternoon, we'd only finished twenty T-shirts, but we'd worked so hard that when Taylor's mom called on their way back into town and invited us to meet for pizza, we jumped at the chance. We stopped by Olivia's so she could quickly feed her bazillion pets, then Mom dropped us off at Payneston

Pizzeria, promising to be back in an hour to get us.

I opened the door of the pizzeria just as someone else was coming out. "Oh!" she gasped, nearly falling over as she juggled the large pizza box in her hands.

I noticed her black boots right away. It was Poinsettia. "Um, hi," I said.

"Hey!" She smiled. "How's it going?"

I wanted to tell her about the ceremony the night before, but it just wasn't the time or place. Especially not when I noticed Kayley's mom sitting right next to Taylor's mom. We weren't the only ones meeting at the pizzeria.

"Great," I said, smiling.

"Have a good night!" she called over her shoulder as she disappeared down the street.

"Who was that?" asked Olivia as the door closed behind us.

"Poinsettia," I whispered. "The stylist who cut and colored my hair."

"Why are you whispering?" Olivia whispered back.

I laughed. "I don't know!"

We hurried over to Taylor, who was waiting for us at a table near her mom's. We asked her about the meet, and told her about our T-shirt-making afternoon.

Meanwhile, Cassidy, Alexis, and Kayley were sitting in a circle of three at their own table, talking and gossiping. They didn't even turn around or acknowledge our presence. So much for ceremonies.

The moms were spilling over, mingling from table

to table, talking. Our table and Cassidy's obviously weren't going to blend.

"Pizzas are on the way," said Taylor's mom, giving us a sympathetic glance. "Here are some quarters."

Taylor, Olivia, and I made a beeline for the Star Wars pinball machine. We took turns playing, laughing at each other and scoring bonus points.

Within minutes, Cassidy, Kayley, and Alexis were standing beside the machine, watching us.

Funny thing, they didn't want to talk to us. They just had to butt in whenever we tried to do something different than them.

"Really. You're still playing that," said Cassidy.

"Actually, I'm still *winning* at it," I said, hoping this would remind her that not that long ago she used to compete right beside me. We'd kept a running tally all through fourth grade.

"I'm so bored," said Alexis, leaning her elbows on the machine and resting her chin in her hands.

"You're blocking my view!" Olivia complained, leaning over her and trying to push her aside.

"I'm just saying, this is so boring compared to last night," Alexis went on.

My eyes widened in surprise. "Why? What was last night?" Did they know about *our* night, what we'd done? But how could they?

"The eighth-grade dance," Kayley said meaningfully.

"Oh, *that.*" I tried to act like it was no big deal to us. "How was it?"

"Oh. My. God. It was so much fun," said Cassidy. "We were there until, like, ten. We danced the entire time."

"How did you get to go?" asked Taylor.

"Everyone on cheer got to," Alexis explained, "because we're, like, important to the football team winning."

Olivia frowned. "That doesn't seem fair."

"No," I agreed. "Not really."

Cassidy shrugged. "You shouldn't have quit, I guess," she said to me.

I just looked at her, trying to figure out what she really meant. "Whatever." She'd never once seemed upset about my quitting before. Maybe she wasn't upset, though; she was too busy gloating. Was I supposed to stay on cheer just so I could go to eighth-grade dances?

"Then how did *you* get in?" Taylor asked Kayley.

"Didn't I tell you? Um, I'm doing some stuff with the cheer squad now. Handsprings and stuff," Kayley explained. "They needed more athletics in their routines."

"Why didn't anyone ask *me*?" Taylor wondered out loud, which was odd, because I didn't think she'd actually be interested. Still, it's nice to be asked, I guess.

Kayley slipped some quarters into the machine and gently made room for herself, where Olivia had been playing. "It's who you know."

I glanced over at our tables, glad to see the pizza

had arrived. The sooner we could eat and not hang out with our former friends, the better. No matter how good we felt, they always found a way to make us feel bad about ourselves.

So far, all we'd gotten out of our Friday night ceremony was new toenail polish.

Chapter 9

On Monday morning, I locked my bike next to Taylor's, and we started walking toward the crowd gathered In front of school, looking for Olivia. For some reason I was spacing out, and at first I didn't notice Bethany Peck, a girl from my homeroom, who was walking beside me.

"Fine, *don't* say hi," she muttered as she passed me—in the kind of way that a person *has* to notice.

"What? Sorry! Hi!" I called after her.

"Whatever!" Bethany called over her shoulder.

"What was that about?" Taylor asked as we looked around for Olivia.

"I spaced and forgot to say hi," I explained. "She took it really personally."

Taylor shrugged. "She's sensitive."

"Not usually," I said. Then again, not only did I sit next to her in homeroom, we were also lab partners in science, so I guess me not saying hi did seem pretty rude.

Olivia ran up to us, panting and out of breath. "So, talk to anyone yet?" she gasped.

"Just Bethany. Why? And what happened, did you run here instead of catching the bus?" I asked.

"No, I'm just—you won't believe it. You will not believe it," she said.

"Especially not if you never tell us what it is!" Taylor said.

"Everyone's talking about it. Everyone," Olivia said. "At the dance Friday night, there was a smoke bomb. A stink bomb. Whatever you call it. The building had to be evacuated at, like, eight o'clock. The dance was basically canceled." She stopped to take a breath. "You know what that means?"

I felt my heart start beating faster. "Cassidy didn't mention that on Saturday night. That means she didn't actually go to the dance. She was faking it!" I cried. In a weird way, that made me very happy.

"Let's go bust them," said Taylor. "Ooh, this is too good to be true." She started toward Cassidy and Alexis, but then stopped and looked at Olivia. "You're sure it's true, right?"

"Yes, I heard about ten people talking about it on the bus," Olivia said. "Listen, if you two aren't *brave* enough, just say so." She started to march toward Cassidy.

We quickly followed her. I walked up to Cassidy and briefly remembered all the things I'd put away—or fanned the flames with—that used to be part of our former friendship.

The flames—wait a second. The fire—the big

whoosh!—had happened just before eight. It had stunk up the whole house. Had the stink bomb happened at the same time? I felt a shiver as I stopped beside Olivia and Taylor. Suddenly I was freezing.

"So," Taylor began, "do you want to tell us more about the eighth-grade dance? And how you danced until ten?"

"What? We never said that!" Cassidy laughed. "Everyone knows the dance got, uh, called off after the electrical thing—"

"Stink bomb," Olivia corrected her. "Smoke filling the gym."

"Right." Cassidy's face turned slightly red.

"What would you know about it, anyway?" asked Alexis. "You were probably home polishing your Girl Scout badges."

"Were not," Olivia said. "Anyway, they're not made of silver. You can't polish cloth. You wouldn't know because you didn't earn any—"

"What *did* you do, then?" Kayley demanded.

"Not much," I admitted. "Watched a movie. Sat around *not* making up phony stories about dances we'd never been to."

"Hey, nice shoes." Cassidy suddenly pointed to the brown-and-pink sneakers I was wearing. She was totally trying to change the subject. "Where'd you get those?"

"See you around," I said, and we kept walking into school.

"That went well," Taylor commented. "Especially considering we totally caught them in a lie."

"She's probably going to mock my shoes later, on the Peeps," I said. "I mean, they've been nice to us before. *Then* remember what happened afterward."

"You guys feel free to be pessimistic. But I, for one, am claiming this as a brand-new Monday," Olivia declared, speaking very clearly. "I wore my Monday underwear and everything. I have to do the morning announcement today. Mr. Brooks gave me a week off to get my pronunciation back, and my time's up. Could one of you come upstairs with me for formal support while I do the broadcast?"

"I think you mean moral support," I said.

"Whatever. *Support*," she urged. "You can make sure Cassidy doesn't pull anything."

"Okay, sure," I said.

We quickly stopped by my homeroom, and Ms. Thibault gave me a hall pass so I could go upstairs with Olivia. She's really cool about things like that—she gets that it's not life or death whether you are in homeroom for attendance and early morning study hall. At the same time, I knew she'd check with Mr. Brooks later on, to make sure I actually did show up at the taping studio like I said I would.

In the studio, Cassidy gave us a sweet smile, like she hadn't totally thrown me under the bus when it was *my* turn to do the morning announcement. She was completely nice to Olivia, helping her get ready, and even warning her when the camera was about to start rolling so she didn't sit there looking into a mirror and trilling about the rain in Maine.

Lucky Olivia.

"Good Monday morning, Panthers! This is Olivia Salinas, with this morning's update," she began. "First, a serious story. As many of you know, at approximately eight o'clock on Friday night, the eighth-grade dance was interrupted—hey, anyone else out there notice all the eights? Go ahead, play the lottery. Eights to win!" She smiled. "Okay, back to serious. The dance was tragically cut short, because I think it only started at seven thirty, not that I'd know because nobody invited me. . . .

"Anyway," Olivia continued, "someone set off a stink bomb. PU. Not as in Payneston University, but as in PU, that really smelled horrible. Or so I heard on the bus. On the plus side, the school found out the sprinkler system works just great."

I thought Mr. Brooks was about to have a panic attack. He looked at Olivia, and then at Cassidy, and then back again, and then over at *me*, like I'd had anything to do with it.

"I didn't write any of that," said Cassidy. "What she's saying?"

"She's kind of a free spirit sometimes," I said quietly.

"Anyone having any information about the stink bomb is instructed to contact Principal Monroe," Olivia continued. "You know, funny thing. I went to a bonfire on Friday night myself. Anyway . . ." She finished the news report and listed off the school events for the day.

"You may have missed the first meeting, but it's not too late to join the Endangered Animals Club," she said. "In fact we're selling T-shirts for just ten dollars each, and they're really cool, each designed by me—"

Since when was it her designs?

"As you may already know, I'm in charge—"

Wait a second, I thought. Wasn't I co-chair?

"So, come to our next meeting, whenever it is, or buy a T-shirt. And on a personal note, anyone who doesn't sign up or get a shirt is just plain ignorant, misinformed, and stupid. Have a great day, Panthers!"

As Cameron shut off the camera, I glanced at Cassidy to gauge her reaction. "It wasn't what I gave her," she said, sounding defensive. "After, uh, last week, Mr. Brooks reviews all the text himself."

Olivia stood up and looked over at me from the news desk. "How'd I do?"

"Um . . ." I shrugged. "Slur much?" I said without thinking. I coughed, hoping to cover up the fact I'd just insulted her.

"What?" Olivia asked. "What did you say?"

"Do you think you could possibly sssslur your esses any more?" I said. Then I put my hand over my mouth.

"Yeah. Not so good." She winced. "But *you* try talking with this stuff in your mouth."

"What?" Mr. Brooks looked so shocked that he was temporarily unable to form sentences. "What was with that last comment? Ignorant and stupid?"

"Oh, that? It was a joke. Ha-ha." Olivia faked a very, very, insincere laugh.

Mr. Brooks frowned. "Miss Salinas, you should know, in fact, it should be ingrained in you, that we don't use those sorts of words in our school."

Olivia nodded. "You're right, I'm sorry. Totally sorry. I guess."

"The whole thing was out of control, out of bounds," Mr. Brooks continued.

The first bell started to ring.

"You'll need to do a makeup broadcast tomorrow with a public retraction of those comments," Mr. Brooks told Olivia.

"A re-whation?"

"Retraction," he said. "It means apology. It means you take back what you said in a very public way."

Olivia let out an annoyed sigh. "Really? You think that's a good idea?"

Mr. Brooks raised his eyebrows. "It's a very good idea, Olivia. I'll see you tomorrow morning."

"Okay, but I think you're being too sensitive," she muttered as we headed out the door.

"And another thing," I said. "What was with saying you were in charge of the club? I'm working with you. We're co-chairs," I added. "'Co' means two, as in cooperating."

"I know what it means," Olivia said. "I may be spacey but I'm not stupid. Why, what did I say?"

"You said, 'I'm in charge.'"

She laughed. "Well, that's dumb. *You're* not in charge. We both are."

I threw up my hands. "That's what I'm trying to tell you!"

The second bell rang just then, and I was glad to slip down the hall into algebra class. How could I argue with Oblivia and win?

"Madison? Madison! Wait up!" Cassidy called after me.

I stopped and glanced back at her. "I don't want to be late to class," I said.

"This will only take a sec," she said.

True. Her insults usually didn't take long. *Here it comes,* I thought. "Yeah?" I asked.

"You know I'm having my big Halloween party Thursday night, right?" Cassidy asked.

"Um . . . yeah," I said slowly, remembering how she'd uninvited me in front of the entire middle school cheerleading squad on that humiliating day a week ago.

"I *really* hope you can come," said Cassidy.

"Really? But you said—"

"Yes, definitely," she said. "Tradition's tradition, right?"

"Right," I said slowly. "I guess." But had tradition meant anything to her lately? I didn't know what to think of her invitation, but I guessed I'd show up and find out. What else would I do on Halloween? "Can Olivia and Taylor come, too?"

"Of course. What a ridiculous question," she scoffed. "Like they wouldn't be invited?"

Either she was starting to have a split personality . . . or maybe our little ceremony had worked some magic, after all. Had she forgotten that we had all been uninvited to the party?

First the stink bomb, now this!

Chapter 10

"Who are *you* supposed to be?" I asked. I had just opened the door to Olivia, who was wearing a green dress, green tights, and a pair of old pink Ugg boots. She had a purse slung across her shoulder, with fake arrows—actually, on closer inspection, they were pens with feathers glued to the tops—sticking out of it.

"Robin Hood. I steal from the rich and give to the poor!" Olivia came inside and closed the door behind her. She looked like a fairy that had gotten kicked out of fairy school. "Really, I just needed to find a costume that I could wear green tights with, because those are the only tights I have right now without holes, and this was all I could come up with. I look silly, I know."

Taylor laughed. "Kind of. Then again, look at me. This costume was my little cousin's last year, but since I'm so short I can wear it. There are some advantages to not growing tall." She twirled around in her Snow White costume, waving her arms in a delicate, graceful, Snow-Whitish way. She wore a black wig that made her hair look like a plastic shell, and a white headband.

I'd improvised at the last minute, turning myself into

a wicked witch with a black cape, a pointed witch's hat, lots of green face makeup, and a carefully positioned fake wart on my nose. I was wearing a wig from my mother's testing days—I think it had been tested on about a thousand times, because the long black hair was as matted as a shaggy dog's.

"Has anyone figured out why Cassidy reinvited us?" Taylor leaned over to fix her shoe, nearly losing her headband and her wig. "I still say they're setting us up for something."

"And I still say you're paranoid," I said. "She seemed genuine when she asked me. And we've always gone to her party. Why would we stop now?"

"Duh. Because she told us flat out last week that she didn't have space for us," said Taylor.

"She must have recalculated. So. Is everyone ready?" I asked.

We picked up our treat bags for collecting candy after the party, and stepped outside into the cool October night. "I can't believe it's nice out," said Olivia. "This is so unexpected."

I gazed up at the clear sky, and the nearly full rising moon.

"Remember last year? It rained and we were completely drenched by the time we got to the party," Taylor said. "Which was not a good look for a girl band."

"Especially not when everyone tried to get us to sing," I said. "Nightmare." I remembered how Cassidy had started a chant, demanding that we sing. We weren't planning on singing. We'd only dressed like we were.

Once we'd escaped that threat, we'd been challenged to play the Rock Band video game, and with Olivia on drums, we didn't stand a chance of winning. So why exactly were we so eager to go back?

"This time there's nothing they can do to embarrass us," Olivia declared. "No more group costumes."

Taylor laughed. "That just means we'll get singled out on our own!"

"I don't know. I don't think that's going to happen," I said.

"Why not?" asked Taylor.

"I just have a feeling. I can't explain it," I said. "Of course, *I'm* not dressed like a miniature Snow White."

We all started laughing so hard that we couldn't stop. We half walked and half skipped over to Cassidy's house, which was only about four blocks away. This seemed so normal, going to Cassidy's for Halloween, like I had every year since I was eight. But a week ago, if someone had told me we'd end up there this Halloween, I'd have said they were crazy.

So who's crazy now? I wondered. *Me for going after I was disinvited, or Cassidy, for re-inviting me?*

As we neared her house, I could see plastic skeleton heads poking onto the ends of Cassidy's front-yard fence posts, and cobwebs draped on bushes and trees. A steady line of guests was filing in, while Cassidy's

88

mother, Amber, was standing outside and handing candy to smaller kids who were trick-or-treating.

"Whoa. Popular much?" asked Taylor.

"Hey, Madison!" Cassidy's mom greeted me. "Taylor, Olivia—it's so nice to see you guys here. Thanks for coming!"

"We wouldn't miss it," I said with a smile, thinking, *We almost missed it, but your daughter did a 180-degree turn.*

We had just walked into the house when Cassidy came to greet us at the door saying, "Welcome, I'm so glad you could come!"

It was like looking into a mirror—a cracked mirror, actually.

Cassidy was standing there dressed in the exact same costume as mine: black cape, green face, black wig, pointed black hat, carefully placed nose wart. "Should one of us have been Glinda, the good witch?" I asked.

Cassidy put her hand over her mouth. "OMG, Madison. Embarrassing."

"For you," I said boldly.

Cassidy took a step back as if this hadn't occurred to her, but now that it had, it was crushing her. "How did you get your skin *that* green?" she asked as she let us into the house.

I waited for the insult to follow. Like: it almost matches the way your hair looked that day. Or: I didn't know you were part alien.

Instead, she said with a sigh, "You're so *good* at makeup."

That was news to me. "I am?" That wasn't what she'd thought last week.

"Yeah. I could never get mine to look as good as yours. Do you think you could help make mine a little better?" she asked.

"Sure, maybe later . . . ," I said, edging away. She was acting a little bit crazy. I didn't know what was going on with her.

"Help yourself to chips, candy, and punch!" Cassidy said. "Plus there are candy apples, caramel apples, bobbing for apples . . ."

"I thought this was a Halloween party, not an apple party," said Olivia.

Cassidy gave an embarrassed laugh. "I didn't realize. Overkill. How stupid of me." She shook her head. "Excuse me for a sec. Mom!" she yelled, marching outside.

We walked through the entryway into the large living room. Bowls of food and punch were set out on a table in front of the kitchen. Dozens of kids from school were milling around, snacking and talking, but it was hard to recognize anyone at first because of the costumes.

A machine sent cloudy wafts of fake smoke across the room, while cans of soda were set out in bowls of swirling dry ice. Strings of black and purple lights dangled over the breakfast bar, while orange and black streamers draped from the ceiling. Every once in a while, a cackling, maniacal laugh could be heard from the stereo speakers. On the coffee table beside me was a vat of disgusting-looking spaghetti brains.

Everything seemed different from the last time I was here—and not just because it was Halloween. The sofa, the paint colors, everything about the room had somehow changed. When was the last time I'd been here?

"See that vampire over there?" Taylor pointed to the bobbing apples. "I think that's Hunter."

"Doesn't he realize he'll lose all his face makeup if he does that?" I said, trying to ignore the fact that he looked cool as a vampire because I still hated him.

Then I realized Cassidy was walking over to join him. Her green makeup might soon be swimming with the apples. I kind of wanted to see that.

While I snacked on candy corn and peanut mix, I saw Cameron dressed as a Red Sox player; there were a couple of lobsters, a waitress, two people dressed as a matching pair of L.L.Bean boots, and lots and lots more vampires.

"Oh, hi, guys!"

I peered at the tiger standing in front of us and recognized Kayley.

"A tiger? Shouldn't you be a kitten?" asked Olivia.

Kayley's whiskers drooped. "What are you saying?"

"Nothing." Olivia shrugged. "You're short and not that tough, that's all."

I laughed, amazed that Olivia had the nerve to say

that. We didn't usually say things like that to the mean girls; they said them to us. Meanwhile, Kayley was falling all over herself complimenting us on *our* costumes, which I knew were not that great. What was going on?

"Is that thing even attached?" Taylor asked. She reached for the wire tail bobbing on the back of Kayley's costume and pulled. The tail came off in her hands.

"Hey!" Kayley said. "Why did you do that?" She grabbed for the wiry tail, but Taylor draped it around her neck, like a scarf.

"It's no big deal. You're just a Maine coon cat now," said Taylor.

"I think you mean a Manx," Olivia said. "Those are the ones without tails. Remember Charlie? He was a foster cat we had for a couple of months?"

I shrugged. It was impossible to keep track of *all* of Olivia's pets, especially the ones her family fostered.

Instead of being angry about the tail thing, all Kayley said was, "I totally admire you for the way you take in and help abandoned animals."

"You do?" asked Olivia. "You never mentioned that before."

"Before what?" asked Kayley.

Alexis walked up, dressed in a mummy costume. "Hi, guys!"

"Hi, mummy," said Olivia, snickering under her breath.

Alexis held out a caramel apple on a small paper plate to Taylor. "Here, Snow White, I brought you an apple. But it's not poisoned, I promise. It's delicious."

"Why would I trust *you*?" asked Taylor, refusing to accept it.

Alexis looked genuinely hurt. "Well, um, do you want something else?"

"No thanks," said Taylor.

"Where's your tail?" Alexis asked Kayley. "What happened?"

"It, um, fell off?" said Kayley.

It was so weird to see them like this. They suddenly had no confidence. At all.

"You guys look *so* cute," Alexis said. "Love the fake arrows," she told Olivia. "And your makeup is priceless!" she said to me, gushing with compliments.

"Your costume must have taken so long to do," Taylor said to her.

"Not really. There's a couple of long pieces, that's all," said Alexis. "And they attach here, with this clip—"

"So if I just pull here . . . wouldn't it all come unraveled?" asked Olivia.

"You wouldn't," said Alexis.

But Olivia already had. The strips of cotton unfurled quickly and dropped to the floor, leaving Alexis standing in the middle of the party in just a goofy pink Care Bears T-shirt, and a pair of black gym shorts that looked a size too small. It was almost as bad as being caught in her underwear.

"Ack!" she screamed. She tried to gather the gauze strips around her waist, but she tripped on them as she fled up the stairs. I thought I saw a couple of camera flashes behind me, like someone was taking her picture.

"Maybe someone will put *that* on the Payneston Peeps," I said to Olivia and Taylor, laughing. "Come on, we'd better get out of here."

"Why? This is fun," said Taylor, grinning from ear to ear. "In fact, I've never *had* so much fun at one of Cassidy's parties."

"I know, right?" Olivia agreed.

We helped ourselves to more treats—Cassidy's mom always had the best collection of Halloween candy—and wandered around, saying hi to people and checking out costumes. We skipped bobbing for apples and headed straight for the *Scream* movie marathon, then after fifteen minutes of that, raced back to the living room when we heard our favorite song.

I couldn't put my finger on it, but there was something sort of "blah" about this year's party. Almost like it had never really gotten started.

"The party's kind of peaked, don't you think? Seems like people are leaving," I said. "We don't want to be the last ones to go."

We started toward the door when suddenly Cassidy reached out and grabbed my sleeve. "You're not leaving, are you? The party's just getting started!" Her green makeup was slightly streaked, and it looked like she'd been crying. Then I remembered she'd gone over to bob for apples.

Behind her was a group of eighth-grade cheerleaders whom I didn't know all that well.

"Can you believe it?" I said to them. "Cassidy copied my costume. Again. In fact, she's always copying me. Of course, our costumes are not exactly the same. Hers is lame, mine is not."

Cassidy's forehead creased in confusion. "How can I have the lamer costume when we have the same costume?"

"Have you seen your face?" I said. "Your wart is drooping." I reached out and plucked it off the end of her nose. "See?"

The other cheerleaders started cracking up and were teasing her as we walked away. As we headed out the door, Amber was walking in.

"Leaving so soon?" she asked.

A group of high school students was out on the sidewalk in front of Cassidy's house. I noticed one of the boys was carrying a carton of eggs.

"Hey—can I have some of those eggs?" I called after him. I glanced back at the front stoop to make sure Cassidy's mom was still inside.

"Sure. Well, wait. How much are eggs a dozen? Couple bucks, right? How many do you want?"

"Four, I guess," I said.

"So, give me two bucks for four."

"That's not fair."

"I have them. You don't. If you don't want any . . ."

"Fine." I pulled two wrinkled dollar bills out of the pocket of the jeans I was wearing under my costume.

I'd never made a deal like this before. It felt kind of like a spy movie: *The Egg Ultimatum*.

We each took an egg from the carton, then I took a second one. "On the count of three," I said, aiming at Cassidy's front door. "One, two—"

Cassidy opened the door.

"Three!" Eggs sailed through the night air like shooting stars. Or, rather, falling meteors. One hit a tree. One splattered on the front steps. One hit the living room window. And one hit Cassidy's hat. Egg yolk dripped down over the brim onto her cape and her face and neck, in gooey strings. Oh, no! Oh, no, Madison!" Taylor cried.

"Sh!" I said.

"I can't believe you just did that!" said Olivia.

"Who's out there?" Cassidy called. I saw her wipe her face with the sleeve of her cape. "Ew!" she screeched.

We took off down the street, laughing. Maybe it was just my costume, but I was definitely feeling wicked.

Chapter 11

When I got home later that evening after trick-or-treating, Mom stood in the doorway with her hands on her hips, like an angry cowgirl getting ready to draw.

And by draw, I don't mean art.

By cowgirl, I mean she was dressed like one for Halloween. She had on a leather vest and chaps. Her cowgirl hat was a size too small and perched on top of her head like a decoration. She didn't look like herself at all.

"Madison? Care to explain?" she asked.

David was standing behind her, looking slightly awkward in a matching cowboy getup that also seemed a size too small, like mom's hat. David's not a small person—he's tall, big, and burly. He and Mom met when he was helping build this house for us.

"Amber just called and said their house had been egged. How did this happen?"

"Um . . ."

"Egged by *you,* I should have said. She heard you, Madison. She heard your voice, and she heard you laughing. You hit Cassidy! I think you know what you need to do now."

I do? I thought.

"Call their house and apologize!" she said as if it were the most obvious thing in the world.

"What? Me? After everything Cassidy's done to me, I have to apologize for this one little teensy thing that is actually a very common prank on Halloween?" I asked. Of course, we'd done some other things, too, but if Mom didn't know, I wouldn't tell her.

"Cassidy never egged our house," Mom said, staring me down. "You need to call Cassidy's house and apologize to her and her mom. And you're grounded for the weekend," Mom said.

"Grounded?" I was stunned. "Really?" I looked over at David, who shrugged, like he wasn't sure about it, either.

"You know where the phone is, Madison. I'll give you one minute to call!" she yelled over her shoulder, opening the door to a group of trick-or-treaters.

I grabbed the phone off the kitchen counter and dialed the number I'd memorized years ago. Cassidy's mother answered. I felt the guilt taking over, making my voice all squeaky and pathetic. "Can I talk to Cassidy?" I asked.

"Sorry, Madison. She's not home."

That didn't make sense. "She's not? What about the party?"

"The party pretty much died after you left, so she

and the other girls went out trick-or-treating," Cassidy's mom said.

What? The party died after *we* left? Since when? Because of the embarrassment that ensued from having an egg on your face and hat? Since when would Cassidy and her friends give up on a party that "everyone" wanted to be at? That was weird.

It's Halloween, I told myself. *The night was created for weirdness.*

"Oh. Well, when she gets back, could you tell her I'm sorry about the eggs?" I said to Cassidy's mom. "And, um, I want to apologize to you, too. I'm sorry. I guess I just got carried away."

"It's not a big deal, Madison. We probably won't even have to clean it off before it rains again and the rain washes it off. I guess that's one of the benefits of living here." She laughed. "But, Madison? Why would you do that to our house? I mean, I get that maybe you and Cassidy aren't close anymore, but are you that far apart?"

"Kind of," I said. "Anyway—I have to go, there's someone at the door," I lied. "Talk to you later!"

After I hung up, I sat on the couch for a minute, not wanting to move because then I'd have to take my costume off. Though I was dying to do that, I also knew it was going to be a lot of work to get rid of all the makeup.

"Hey." Parker sat down beside me on the couch, his scary white *Scream* mask pushed up on his head.

"Since when do you do Halloween pranks?"

I shrugged. "It was just a few eggs."

"What were you trying to do, act like your costume?" he asked.

Our gray tabby cat, Rudy, ran out from under the sofa, where he'd been hiding due to the constant ringing of the doorbell. Rudy doesn't tolerate guests well. Or costumes. He took one look at me and Parker and raced away, his nails scrabbling on the wood floor, bolting for the stairs.

"So why Cassidy's house? I thought you wanted her out of your life."

"I did," I said. "I mean, I do."

"So . . . why would you go to her house for a party and then egg it afterward? That doesn't make sense," said Parker, dumping a pillowcase full of candy onto the sofa.

I took off my pointy hat and set it on his head. "When you're older, you'll understand. Life is complicated."

"Ooh, deep. Maybe I could take you seriously if you weren't dressed like a character from *The Wizard of Oz*."

"And maybe I could take you seriously if you weren't *ten*," I said.

Before he could continue to torment me, I ran upstairs to the bathroom and locked the door. I thought it'd take a long time to get all the face makeup off, but I used face cream and it slid right off with a couple of tissues.

Life was suddenly so much easier. So I was grounded for a few days. So what? I'd already done what I wanted to do. Ruined Cassidy's Halloween party for her. Finally, my friends and I were coming out on the right side of things for a change.

I pictured the look on Cassidy's face and smiled. Now she knew how it felt, being all alone, wishing she could count on a former friend.

Chapter 12

"This is Olivia Salinas, with this morning's update. Partly sunny tomorrow, with a ninety percent chance of rain." Olivia paused. "How is that *partly* sunny? And how is a ninety percent chance of rain even a *chance*? That seems more like a given. You know?

"Okay, okay! Before I get started with today's update, I need to apologize for my last update. I guess. Though I really don't think I did anything wrong. Oh, right. Sorry, Mr. Brooks. Sorry I used the words *ignorant* and *stupid*. Those are horrible words. Never do it again. Does that count? Okay, great."

I had to smile as I watched Olivia breeze through her on-air apology, otherwise known as her retraction, or, as she put it, her "re-whation."

"Now, moving on . . . well, we've got the usual assortment of exciting news," Olivia continued. "Today's lunch, everyone? Tacos with refried beans. Because what we all need to get through the day is a good dose of heartburn."

Uh-oh, I thought. I glanced around my homeroom to see how everyone else was reacting.

They were actually watching. They were laughing. And not at her—*with* her.

At least it will keep me awake in social studies, because lately it's been soooo boring." She smiled at the camera. "Not that the cafeteria's tacos include anything actually spicy. Speaking of which, you want some good tacos? Come down to the Whale on Friday nights for fish tacos. When you combine my dad's Mexican recipes with fresh fish and shellfish, yum. Tell him I sent you and he'll throw in a free side of lime tortilla chips and salsa.

"What's that?" Olivia glanced to the side. "Oh, sorry, Mr. B. Didn't mean to do an on-air ad. Right. Bad call. In other announcements, the cheer squad will be selling discount coupons to the water park. The soccer team is going to sectionals, blah blah blah . . . Can anyone actually sit through a soccer game? I'm just asking. My sister Laney—okay, she's only eight, she's good and all, but my butt goes numb sitting there waiting for someone to score a goal—

"I can't say 'butt'? Seriously?

"Well, okay. Looks like time is running out, and like I said, most of this isn't important. I can skip it." She shuffled through the papers in front of her, then set them down on the desk and faced the camera again. "Basically, it's a slow news day. But today at lunch, the Endangered Animals Club will be selling our custom T-shirts. Only eighty-nine left. You *really* want one of these. If you don't get one, you'll regret it. One, it's a great cause, as we all know. And two, anyone who doesn't have one is going to look like an idiot. That's all there is to it. So don't be idiotic.

"What's that, Mr. Brooks? Oh. I did? What did I say? Oh. Well, have a great day, Panthers, and it looks like you'll be seeing me again tomorrow." She smiled, showing her braces in a lopsided grin that seemed to be sort of gloating. "Go ahead, look forward to it. I know I will."

Some people in homeroom applauded, while I had kind of a queasy feeling in my stomach. Olivia wasn't acting like herself. Or was this her new self? Was she going to start acting as dramatically as she sometimes dressed?

"Quiet down, everyone, quiet down," Ms. Thibault said.

"I didn't know she was so funny," said Justin Stahlman, who sat to my right.

"I know, right?" Bethany commented from my left. "You're so *lucky* to be such good friends with her."

"Dude, she's hilarious," said Justin. "She should do the news every day."

"I have a feeling she probably will," I said with a slight smile.

Halfway through math class, I felt Hunter's hot breath on my neck. Nothing unusual about that, but today, I just didn't feel like I had to sit there and take it.

I was about to turn around and tell him to breathe

elsewhere when he leaned forward, so he was looking over my shoulder. Not just looking over—his chin was practically perched on my shoulder.

"Madison?" he asked sort of in a whisper. "Madison?"

"That's my name. What seems to be the problem?" I asked. I wasn't sure I'd ever been that close to a boy before, not counting wrestling with my brother. I wasn't sure if I liked it or hated it.

But I did know that it made me very self-conscious about my neck. Was it a normal neck? Was it too big, too small, too . . . necky?

Maybe it was irresistible. Maybe I needed to start wearing shirts with collars—no, turtlenecks—from now on, if this was the way Hunter acted when I sat in front of him. I still felt sort of naked without my long hair going down my back.

"You smell . . ."

I braced myself.

"Nice," he said.

I let out my breath. "Really?"

"Yeah. So, uh, can I look at your work?" he asked. "I can't figure out what he's talking about."

I sighed. "What else is new?" I pushed my paper over on my desk and leaned out of the way so that he could get a good look at it.

"What's the deal with that?" Hunter pointed to question number three.

"Did you not take sixth grade?" I asked him.

"What?"

"That's an equation. E-quay-zhun," I said slowly. "Remember, when you see it, you know that you're supposed to solve for x."

Hunter looked like he was in pain, like he needed to summon the school nurse. The school pre-algebra nurse.

"You do okay in your other classes, right?" I asked.

He nodded.

I tapped my pencil against his desk. "So how can you be so stupid in this class?"

"Don't say that. *Stupid* is not a good word."

Great, now I was turning into clueless Olivia, insulting people right and left. "I'm sorry. Sorry! I didn't mean—"

"Look, just because you're good at something, doesn't mean you can make fun of people who aren't."

"I know, I know." I nodded. "I'm sorry." I paused, trying to think of the right thing to say. "But you really don't get any of this, and you're slowing down our entire class, and—" I put my hand over my mouth. What was I doing? "You are hopeless about algebra." I gulped. How had that slipped out?

"Well." He sat back in his chair, crossed his arms, and gave me a smug look. "At least I'm *nice*. Which is more than I can say for you." He shoved my chair forward with his feet.

I let that sink in for a moment or two, as I thought about the way Hunter usually dealt with me. "Hold on.

Since when are you nice?" I asked him. "One time you told me I looked like a hedgehog."

"I did not," he said.

"Did too," I argued.

He glared at me. "Must have been the hair on your neck," he said.

"Yeah, well." I felt my face burning. "I bet a hedgehog could multiply better than you can."

Chapter 13

I decided not to tell Olivia and Taylor what had happened with Hunter, because I was actually sort of embarrassed about it. Maybe he was a royal jerk, but since when did I insult people for not understanding math? He'd said I wasn't nice, which was true, and the fact that Hunter Matthews could be right about something meant the world was upside down.

I took my plate of tacos and headed over to the east wall, under the PANTHER PRIDE—100 YEARS STRONG! banner, where we had set up a table to sell shirts during lunch.

"So, Olivia. How many more days do you think you're going to be doing the morning announcement?" I asked. "A week's worth? A month's worth?"

I couldn't help noticing that as we carried our trays toward our table, people were glancing up from their lunches to give her high fives and nod or say hello.

"Who knows?" she said. "Mr. Brooks says I'm controversial. What does that mean?"

"That you create controversy. You cause problems." I set my tray down and scooted into a seat next to

Taylor. "Which tends to happen when you call people 'stupid idiots.'"

"What? I never said that!" Olivia took a sip from her glass of water, then turned to her tacos. "This food needs a serious amount of salsa."

"Yes, you did say that. Not all together at the same time, but it still counts," Taylor said. "Do you want a summary of all the insults you delivered?" She smiled.

"There isn't enough time, is there?" I said. Just then, Kristie Yamakn, a friend of Taylor's from gymnastics, came up to our table.

"Hey, Taylor," she said. "I thought maybe I could help out—you know, be a new club member?"

"Oh. Well, sorry, but there's no room," Taylor said abruptly.

"I can get another chair," Kristie said. She set down her tray, looking around for a free seat. Our cafeteria's really a zoo for the thirty-seven minutes they give us to eat lunch.

"Yeah, but there still wouldn't be room, because look at this table, it's not big enough, and we need room to put the shirts, so . . ." Taylor looked up at her and shrugged. "Sorry."

"You could make room." Kristie stared at her. "What is with you lately? Did you start another new club or something?"

"What do you mean?"

"A club for rude and annoying people." Kristie picked

up her tray and stomped off across the cafeteria to find another place to sit.

"See you at the gym!" Taylor called after her.

"What's with her?" Olivia asked.

Taylor crunched a carrot. "Supersensitive. She's always been that way. I didn't mean to be rude and annoying, like she said," she said. "It just sort of squeaked out. But really, is there room here? I don't think so."

Suddenly there was a high-pitched squeal, followed by a loud crash. Everyone in the cafeteria stopped talking, eating, or moving.

It was Alexis. She'd been walking over to the cheerleader table when she slipped. Her tray had smashed up against her body, then dropped to the ground and landed on her shoes, covering them with shredded lettuce and chopped tomatoes. Salsa clung to her shirt. A pool of soda spread out under her feet.

Alexis was standing with her hands in the air, staring at her spilled tray and her jeans, which were now splattered with soda and salsa.

No one went to help her. Not even Cassidy, or anyone else from their table. Instead, they started applauding. Standing and applauding, with us.

"Is it wrong that I enjoyed that? Because I really enjoyed that," Olivia said.

Alexis scurried out of the cafeteria, running for cover.

"She totally needs one of these," said Olivia, patting the pile of T-shirts for sale.

"Yeah, we should find her and give her one," I said.

"Yeah. But let's not," said Taylor. "She can buy one if she wants."

"Wait a second," Olivia said. "Is it because of us she just did that?"

"Obviously that had nothing to do with us." Taylor tossed a straw wrapper onto the floor. "They're over there. *We're* over here. It's scientifically impossible for us to have made that happen."

"Okay, but what about the broken plate last Friday night?" Olivia asked. "I dropped it, and she just dropped a tray."

"Oh, that? That's just a coincidence. It's not like we have any actual powers. Come on, Olivia. You're being ridiculous," said Taylor.

"Right. I mean, probably. I know. It's just . . . weird, don't you think?" she asked.

"The tray probably just came out of the dishwasher and was wet. Her hands slipped. End of story," Taylor said.

Right. End of story.

But it still seemed like quite a coincidence.

Chapter 14

"Are you hurt?"

I found Cassidy in the gym on Tuesday after school. She was sitting on the bleachers while the rest of the cheer squad was taking turns on the trampoline, doing flips, laughing, and having fun.

I'd been avoiding her. I didn't feel like apologizing. She'd been mean to me so many times and had never apologized afterward—instead, she usually rubbed it in so that I felt even worse. So why did I have to be the one who apologized?

"Why are you watching instead of jumping?" I asked. "Because you're injured?"

She shook her head. "No." She stretched out her legs on the step below her, rubbing her muscles as if to keep them warm.

"Oh. Well, that's good," I said. "I guess. Are you just taking a break, then?"

"Not by choice," she said. "I'd rather be injured than be in the position I'm in now." She directed a glare across the gym at her teammates and coach. I didn't really want to get into it with her.

"So, I don't know if your mom gave you the message or whatever. But I'm sorry about Halloween. Everything that happened," I said.

"What happened? Oh, wearing the same costume?" She laughed. "Well, that's not your fault."

"Okay, but . . . we kind of egged your house. And got egg on your, uh, face. And hat."

"That was you?" she asked, looking stunned for a second.

I was just as surprised—why hadn't her mom told her? I shrugged. "Yeah. It was me. Sorry."

"No worries," she said, as if it were no big deal to get egg on her nose. "I thought I heard you guys. Anyway, it was Halloween. Things like that are supposed to happen."

"Right. I guess. Sorry," I repeated. I couldn't understand why she wasn't more furious with me.

She sighed, slumping back on the bleachers. "That's the least of my problems right now."

She was obviously dying to talk about it, so I gave in. "Why, what's going on?" I asked. "Why aren't you over there?"

"I got replaced, okay? I got demoted. To junior cheer. Which is not, like it sounds, for high school juniors. It's sixth graders," she explained.

"I know," I said. "We used to be on it together, remember?"

"Right. Right! Of course," she said. "Sure."

"Well, how did it happen?" I asked. "I mean, isn't

there a chance you could change things?"

"I got into an argument with Ms. Throgfeld. She said I had too much of an attitude and I needed to be in the back row for the next game, with the other sixth graders." She shuddered. "The back row," she repeated, slowing to emphasize each word.

I remembered hating the fact that we were hidden, that we were just sort of backups to the older girls in front.

"I just got used to the front, you know? Then, as if that wasn't bad enough, she said I had to be at the bottom of the pyramid. I said, 'I'm not going to be the bottom of the pyramid,' and she said, 'You're too tall now to be the one on top, so remember this is a team and we make team decisions.'"

"Maybe she meant decisions in the best interests of the team?" I suggested.

But Cassidy continued to rant. She was biting her thumbnail while she talked, which made it a little hard to understand her. "Too tall. As if. I'm only five three. Where's the logic in that? What am I going to do? Getting tossed in the air was my trademark thing."

I couldn't remember the last time Cassidy had asked me for advice. "Um, you'll teach the younger girls how to do things. Be their leader."

"Take me to your leader," Cassidy said in a robotic voice, speaking as though she were an alien from outer space.

"That's not funny," I said. "Actually, thinking back, you never were all that funny."

She looked at me, blinking back tears. "Harsh."

"Teasing, I was teasing," I said.

"It's okay, I deserve it." Her shoulders sank.

"You know, if this doesn't work out, you could join the Endangered Animals Club. Except that we actually don't need anyone right now—"

Just then, Ms. Throgfeld shouted, "Cassidy, over here, now! We need you!"

Cassidy jumped down from the bleachers and did a couple of handsprings over to the coach, obviously trying to impress her. She misjudged the amount of room she had and went cartwheeling off the mat, crashing into the wall on the other side of the gym.

Ms. Throgfeld shook her head as Cassidy stood up, looking slightly crumpled and blushing. "Never mind, go sit back down. I don't know *how* you'll be ready for the game Friday night."

"I can do it!" Cassidy said. "I can do anything you want. Really, just ask!"

Ms. Throgfeld glanced over at me. "Madison, maybe you could talk to her about teamwork, about having the right attitude."

"Me?" The person who Ms. Throgfeld had told not to bother with cheer if I wasn't invested in it a hundred percent? I was the last person who should be talking about teamwork. And hadn't Cassidy just offered to

do whatever she wanted? Was Ms. Throgfeld even listening to her?

"No, I don't think so—sorry, I have to get going," I said, slowly backing away. I didn't want to get any more involved with this than I already was.

When I got home, there was a message from Taylor, asking me to call her immediately. When I did, she sounded hysterical. "This is weird, okay? Really, really weird. You won't believe what happened. I said something to Kayley while she was doing a flip on the balance beam, and she fell off!"

"What did you say?" I asked.

"Just her name!" Taylor said.

"Did she get hurt?" I asked. I hated to admit it, but I almost liked the thought of Kayley having a mishap—as long as she wasn't seriously hurt. She always made such a big deal out of being so good at gymnastics. It was annoying.

"No, she didn't get hurt then, but—"

"That's great!" I said.

"No, it's not great! Listen, that's not all that happened," Taylor said. "I was trying to make up for causing her slip on beam by cheering *extra* hard for her when she did her bars routine, but somehow I yelled, 'Watch out, Kayley!' I broke her concentration, and she slipped and fell then, too. So now she has a sprained wrist and she's completely *out* of competition for at least a couple of weeks."

"Oh. That's not good." *Or is it?* I wondered.

"No. I tried to apologize but I ended up telling her that her timing was off. Madison? What's going on? It's like I say things that I don't mean, and I can't help it. Nothing I say is coming across right. Now other people are getting hurt," Taylor said, "because of us."

"Taylor, listen to yourself. Do you really think that you had anything to do with Kayley slipping off the balance beam or bars?" I asked. "I mean, that happens all the time, right?"

"Not with Kayley! And you know what I think? It's the stuff we got rid of at your house that night. We have to get it back. My Shawn Johnson pendant—I need it."

"But that's only a good-luck charm—"

"I need it," Taylor repeated. "Okay? Please, Madison."

"Sure. Okay." I'd never heard calm, logical Taylor sound so worried before. "I'll find that box. We'll take everything out of storage and put it back where it was."

She sighed. "Call me when you find it and I'll come over."

"Right. I'll call in a few minutes." I hung up the phone in the kitchen and went straight out to the garage.

I nearly tripped on a ladder that had been left in front of the minivan. Why was there a ladder in front of the shelves?

When I looked up, I saw why. The shelves were empty. The garage had never looked cleaner. All the boxes with extra products? Gone. All the boxes of excess nail polish? Gone. Vamoose. History. And with them, our own, very historical, once-upon-a-time-we-were-friends box. Nowhere in sight. Vanished into thin, stale garage air.

I rushed back inside and found my mom in her office, which was looking equally sparse. "Mom? What happened to all the stuff we kept in the garage?" I asked.

"Oh, that? I'm getting ready for a new phase in my career, so I wanted to throw out the things I didn't need anymore, to open up the space for new projects."

I really didn't need her granola-speak at a time like this. "But where did you *put* everything?"

"Well, some of it went to recycling, some went to hazardous waste, and some was donated to charity . . ."

"Charity? But what about me?"

"Why, what do you need? If it's a product, look no further." She opened the walk-in closet in her office to show me shelves of shampoos, conditioners, and various other hair treatments. "How about some Refreshing Raspberry Rain Shower Rinse? You look a little stressed."

I laughed, feeling out of control. "Yeah. You could say I'm stressed. I had left something in the garage—in a box. It's gone now. And I really, really need it back."

"Oh. Did you have something important in there?"

Would I say I really, really needed something

*un*important back? "Yeah." I laughed again, sounding borderline crazy. "You could say that."

"Well, I'm sorry. I didn't know." She shrugged, all innocent-like.

"You should have asked!" I said.

"Fine, but since when do you store anything in the garage?"

She had a point. I hated that she was taking the fire out of my argument.

"What was it, anyway? What was in the box?" Mom asked.

"Just some old things. Prized possessions." *Apparently ones that possess magical, mystical powers.* "Don't worry about it."

"Oh. Well, let me know if I can help," she said.

I wish you could, I thought as I went back to the kitchen. *I don't know if anyone can.* I drummed my fingernails against the counter.

If we couldn't get our time capsule back, what would we do? I had to think of another way out of this. Right then, I had no idea what to do, except take a deep breath and dial Taylor's number. "I can't find it," I said when she answered.

"What?"

"But I'm still working on it and—"

"*What* did you just say? You can't find it?" Taylor asked. "What kind of idiot would lose something that important?"

"*I* didn't lose it," I said. "It was my mom. She—"

"Oh, sure, blame it on your mom, like everything," said Taylor. "What kind of friend are you, anyway, if you can't hold on to important stuff for me?"

"I'll fix it!" I said, stung by her anger.

We were talking to each other like we hated each other. Like we were . . . mean girls.

Chapter 15

I rushed into Combing Attractions, dripping wet, hands frozen from clutching my handlebars, and completely out of breath. It was five minutes to closing time. I shook off my sopping wet raincoat and hung it on one of the oversize combs.

Inside the salon, Poinsettia was working on an older woman's hair, running the blow-dryer, which was so loud she didn't hear me come in. When she stopped to put the finishing touches on her client's hair, she noticed me and walked over.

"What can I help you with? Your cut and color still look great. Time for an updo?" she asked. "Is there a special occasion coming up? Maybe a school dance?"

"Hardly. More like a redo," I said. "Anyway, it's a little late for an updo, since you chopped my hair into a bob."

She looked a little shocked by my tone—shocked, and annoyed. "You underestimate my considerable powers. I could give you an updo. You wouldn't even know what hit you, it would look so good, so fast."

"Hm," I murmured. "Aren't you about to close, anyway?"

"Sure, I guess, but I'm always willing to make exceptions for special clients. Well, then, what *are* you here for?"

"I need help," I said.

"Honey, you and me both. I'm shorthanded here today. Or should I say short-scissored." She glanced back at her client, an elderly woman with curly white hair. "Tell you what. I'll finish up with her and then we'll talk. Have a seat."

I did, and sifted through the magazines stacked on the table: *Cat Fancy*, *Fortune Tellers Monthly*, and *Mysterious Times*.

What was with this collection? Hadn't Poinsettia ever heard of *People*, or *Glamour*? How about a copy of *Entertainment Weekly*?

In a few minutes, she finished the elderly woman's blow-out, and the older woman paid her bill and collected her coat. "You're smart to wait. Stick with her," she advised me as she zipped up. "Best stylist this town's had in forty years."

"Really?"

"Really." She tied a paisley scarf loosely over her hair. "Take care now," she said as she opened the door and exited into the rainy, windy late afternoon.

I walked over to Poinsettia, who was busy sweeping up. "Okay. So remember when you were coloring my hair, and you were telling that other girl about cutting connections to an old boyfriend?"

"Me? No, I don't think that would have been me."

"Yes, it was!" I said. "The day of that rainstorm."

She rolled her eyes. "Be more specific. Notice how it rains here nearly every day? Well, every day it doesn't *snow*." She laughed and patted her chair. "Have a seat and refresh my memory, why don't you?"

"Right. I came in with green hair and told you I wanted to go in a new direction. While you were coloring my hair, you talked about writing a letter to that girl's old boyfriend and burning it, along with his name."

"Oh, *that*," she said slowly, tapping her nails against the desk. "I guess."

How could something so crucially important to me be like a blip on her radar screen? "How old are you, anyway?" I asked. "Your memory's not great, is it?"

"Look. Why don't you tell me your problem and quit being rude at the same time? And if this is going to take more than five minutes, you need to make an appointment for tomorrow," she said, glancing at the clock, which was shaped like a movie reel.

"Fine, okay." I spun around in the chair to face her. "I didn't mean to be rude. I'm sorry if everything sounds that way. That's just how it is with me right now," I explained. "It's like I start to say one thing, but something else comes out." I shook my head. "I actually don't even know how it happens."

"Maybe you should think about seeing a profes- sional," she suggested. "You know, a therapist."

"I don't need a therapist!" I cried. "If anything, I need a psychic." I looked meaningfully at her. "Someone who's good at uncasting spells. That sort of thing."

Poinsettia held up her hands, scissors aloft. "I cut hair. I can teach you how to apply makeup and I'm very good at manicures. That's it. I'm no psychic."

"Please," I said. "We went overboard. We burned our former friends' names in the fireplace. We threw out some stuff we used to share with them—you know, like, mementos. Now their lives are disasters, and we've turned mean. What should we do?"

"Why should you do anything?" she replied. "That's what you wanted, right?"

"Yes," I said. "No! We didn't want to turn *into* them!"

"Okay then. It's simple. You put too much negativity into the atmosphere. You have to put something positive out there now. You've heard of karma, right?"

"Kind of," I said. "My mom used to have a calendar, I think. She kept track of when good things happened, or she did good deeds—"

"Exactly. And yours is down here." She pressed the chair lever with the toe of her black boot, and I dropped a foot. "Ground level."

"You know, that kind of hurt." I rubbed the back of my neck. "Okay. So maybe we did bring bad luck on ourselves by trying to hurt them. How do we get the good karma back?"

"Simple. Be more than nice to them. Maybe they're just the same as always deep down inside. What you need to do is get to know them better, find out why they're doing the things they're doing."

I raised my eyebrow and looked at her. "I know the answer to that. It's because they're mean. Deep down inside. Even if they're temporarily not, and we are. They're still the same people who make fun of us— they're just taking a break."

"Nobody ends up mean without a pretty good reason," she said. "You're going to have to go back to them, to reach out to them."

"Reach out . . . to *them*?" I wrinkled my nose.

She nodded. "Yes. Exactly."

I didn't want to think about groveling to them. "Really? Are you sure?"

"Well, it depends. Do you want to go through life with bad karma, having everyone dislike you?"

"It's not *everyone*," I argued. "Just most people." I pondered that for a minute. "My cat still likes me. I think."

"Good luck going through life talking to your cat," she said. "That can get you put in the loony bin real fast. I have a great-aunt like that. She's locked up in Augusta now."

"Well, it's your fault if I do end up there. You're the one who mentioned the stupid name-in-flames idea," I reminded her.

She raised her eyebrow. "Do you expect to get back your good karma by talking like that?"

"Sorry," I said. "And, um, how do you get your

eyebrows to look so dramatic? I love that. Of course, it's a little *too* dramatic, really. Maybe you shouldn't have plucked all—"

"It's time to close up for the night," she said, gently guiding me by my shoulders toward the door. "Think about what I said."

Chapter 16

There's not a lot you can't work out over a basket of French fries at the Whale.

At least, that's what I used to think.

"You're late," said Taylor.

"Sorry."

"What's with those jeans? They're so skinny," Olivia commented as I walked closer to the table where she and Taylor were waiting for me.

"Maybe they are skinny, but this is how people wear them in New York," I said in my defense. Was it me, or were they almost identically dressed? Taylor was wearing a typical Taylor gym outfit—fitted black yoga pants, patterned tank top underneath a zip-up hoodie jacket, and a pair of suede slides. And now Olivia, instead of being quirky and interesting, looked exactly the same, except she was about six inches taller and wore pink Crocs.

"New York." Taylor gave an exaggerated sigh. "Oh, please. Give me a break. I've heard enough about you and New York to last my entire life. You don't even go there very much, okay? And who's ever heard of that place?" She pointed to my T-shirt.

"Nobody. That's what makes it cool," I said. "At least I try to be original. At least I'm not a clone."

"What's *that* supposed to mean?" Olivia demanded.

Wow. The three of *us* couldn't even talk now without insulting each other.

I cleared my throat. "Let's start over. The reason I asked you guys to meet me here . . . well, it's probably pretty obvious," I said.

"You desperately need a social life?" asked Taylor. "And you feel terrible that you sold my Shawn Johnson pendant?"

"I didn't sell it!" I said. "My mom gave it away."

"Right. Sure." Taylor rolled her eyes.

"Ever since we had that sleepover and tried to break all our connections to the mean girls, our lives have been a disaster."

"They have?" asked Olivia. "Mine hasn't been. I'm in charge of the newest, most popular club at school—"

"Olivia, you and I are co-chairs," I said. "Have you forgotten?"

"Now the Recycling Club wants me to run their club, too." Olivia dragged a fry through a pool of ketchup. "You know, I'm not sure what you're so worried about. I'm on TV every morning, I know more people at school than I ever did before—"

"And I've never had a better week. I'm the top gymnast on our club right now. It feels great," added Taylor.

"Okay," I said. "Maybe there are some things to like. Cassidy's been demoted at cheer, Kayley has a sprained wrist. Alexis can't make it across the lunchroom without dropping her tray. She'll have to start bringing her lunch."

I continued. "Now, we might have thought all this was really great, you know, a couple of weeks ago, when things were really bad and I was publicly humiliated. Repeatedly. But do we really want to get ahead in life only because other people are miserable? That makes us as bad as the mean girls," I said. "Or worse, even."

"It does?" asked Olivia.

"Well, yeah," I said.

"On the plus side, it's making me really popular," she said, almost bouncing on her seat. "I know a lot more people than I used to. People come up and compliment me. Me! Which they should, you know."

She sounded so much like Alexis and Kayley that I had to cringe.

"In a way, everything's been fine. Everything's been great," Taylor argued. "Nobody's made fun of us, nobody's pulled pranks on us . . . I mean, honestly. Do I have to remind you how bad things were, Madison? Chocolate bra, anybody?"

I blushed at the memory. "No, I remember. I remember that very clearly. But things are even worse now, don't you think?" I asked. "I don't know what's going on, if it's something supernatural or coincidental or what. But I think we have to try to undo what we did."

"*Undo?*" asked Olivia, as if it were the craziest idea in the world. "How? Why?"

"Because, don't you see? We're turning out to be just like them. Do we want that?" I asked. "That's not what we wanted when we started out. We just wanted to cut our connections to them, not switch places with them."

Olivia swished a fry back and forth on her plate. "True. I guess."

"I have been kind of worried about Kayley. It's not like I wanted to ruin her whole season," admitted Taylor.

"And as much as I'm glad Cassidy got what was coming to her, I think it's enough already. So I've been thinking . . ." I paused, unsure. "I don't know, but I guess we have to have another ceremony. And I think in order to make it work, we'll have to invite the original mean girls. OMG," I said.

"Yeah, exactly!" Olivia agreed. "OMG, we can't. Because if we invite them we'll have to confess what we did, and that will be a total disaster, and they'll make things even worse for us than they were before."

"No. As in, OMG are the initials for Original Mean Girls," I explained.

"Oh. Well, OMG OMG then." Olivia laughed.

"You're crazy," said Taylor. "Invite them? They won't hang out with us."

"Sure they will. They want to talk to us right now. They're dying to, in fact," I said.

"True," Olivia said.

"You know what? It wasn't just the ceremony that started throwing things off. Your dumb haircut started everything," said Taylor. "Don't you think? It was the haircut, and then you got the idea from that stylist to have the ceremony and burn names—"

"Wait. That's it. The haircut," I said. "And Poinsettia, too—she was key. Poinsettia said we needed to reach out."

"Who's Poinsettia?" asked Olivia.

"Olivia, she just said it was *her* salon," said Taylor. "But seriously. You're getting all your advice from a hairstylist?"

"Beauty consultant. And she's kind of, like, a friend," I said. "Sort of. Anyway, I have an idea. What if we offer to take them all out for manicures?"

"I don't get it. How will that help?" asked Olivia.

"It's called a mani-*cure*. Cure. Get it?" I said. "It'll fix things."

"Actually, it would make more sense if it was called a girlicure," Taylor said.

I thought about it for a minute. All of a sudden, the perfect word came to me. "No, no—we'll call it a meanicure!" I cried.

"We will?" asked Taylor.

"Yes, it's the perfect name for what we're trying to do," I said.

"Seriously? You think that's perfect?" asked Olivia in a condescending tone.

"Well, at least I don't believe in voodoo dolls," I shot back.

The three of us glared at each other. There we were again: the mean girls in the room. *Us*. OMG.

"Where do we have the mani—*meanicure*?" Taylor asked at last. "The mall?"

I shook my head. "No. I know just the place. Combing Attractions."

Taylor rolled her eyes. "What kind of a name is that? How ridiculous."

"Are you sure about this?" Olivia asked.

"I have to be, I guess," I said. "Anyway, it's the place where I got my haircut, remember?"

"Who's going to invite all of them? And who's going to pay for it all?" asked Olivia. "I don't have any extra money sitting around."

Taylor chimed in. "Neither do I. And I don't have time to figure this out—I have a meet to practice for."

"Well, *I'm* super busy organizing our next fund-raiser," said Olivia. "You're on your own."

It seemed like we should be working on this together. Was this what happened when your karma went down to a subzero level? "Don't worry, I'll take care of everything," I said.

"Don't screw it up, like you screwed up the Endangered Animals Club," Olivia said.

"How did I . . ." My voice trailed off. There was no point arguing anymore.

Chapter 17

"Okay, I just called Combing Attractions and talked to Poinsettia, and we set up a time," I said when we met in the cafeteria for lunch the next day. It seemed like almost everyone around us was wearing one of our club T-shirts. We'd been selling more and more T-shirts all week; our supply was nearly out. "She said we could do it whenever we wanted. I told her Saturday at two o'clock. Isn't that great?"

Olivia had set up a table to sell our remaining tees, and Taylor and I were supposed to help.

"Hm," said Taylor while she folded T-shirts into neat stacks.

"Thrilling," said Olivia.

"And I made some invitations, too. Do you guys want to go hand them out while I sit here and man the table for a while?" I offered.

"Um . . . I don't think so," said Taylor.

"There's not really room for you," Olivia added.

"But I—I started this club with you," I said. "I designed the shirts with you."

They just looked at me as if I were some stranger.

I threw up my hands. "Fine, I'll go invite them to the meanicure." Why did I have to do everything?

As I crossed to the other side of the cafeteria, where the cheerleaders were holding a bake sale, Kayley came in, carrying a plate of baked goods with her uninjured hand.

When she saw me headed her way, she dropped the plate, which smashed into pieces. Cookies rolled across the floor.

She ran back out the door, while I walked up to Cassidy, Alexis, and the other cheerleaders.

There was no line at their table. They wouldn't need the cookies Kayley had just dropped.

I stood there for a minute, evaluating my choices: undercooked lemon bars that oozed lemon filling onto the plate, or vanilla cupcakes with brown charred circles around the outside edges.

"They look bad, don't they?" said Cassidy. "They look terrible."

"No, not at all. I'll buy a cupcake," I said.

"Great!" Alexis grinned. "Fifty cents. Thanks *so* much."

There was a loud, sad clink as the two quarters I'd given her hit the bottom of the can.

"So the reason I'm here," I said, shifting the cupcake in my hand so I could give them the invitations, "is this."

Cassidy and Alexis each scanned their invitations.

"There's an extra one, for Kayley, if you could give it to her," I said.

"We'll give it to her later," said Cassidy. She kept skimming. "*That* place? You want to meet there?"

"It has a great atmosphere. Ambience," I explained.

"Whatever."

"You got your haircut there, didn't you?"

"Mm-hm." I nodded. I wanted to say, *Don't you remember? You wrote a blog post about it. You said I lost my best feature, remember?*

"It really is a great cut for you," said Cassidy. "Totally shows off your cheekbones. It must have taken a lot of courage to do that. Your mom always wanted you to keep your long hair, but you just chopped it off, and it looks ten times better than before."

What was I supposed to say? That I wanted her to not like my haircut, or anything about me, because the fact she did was sort of creepy. I thought it was just more evidence we needed to change.

"Maybe I'll get my hair cut the same way!" Cassidy said.

"What? No! I mean, um, think about it for a while first," I said. "'Cause, you know. Trust me. It's going to take a long time to grow back."

"True. Well, if they do good haircuts, they probably know how to do good manicures," Cassidy reasoned.

"Exactly. So, okay, you guys will come, right? You'll be there?" I asked.

"Sure!" said Alexis.

"And it'll be our treat," I announced.

"Why? That's silly. We'll treat," said Cassidy.

"*No!* No, you can't. I have a, um, gift card. It's cool." I smiled nervously. I didn't have to tell her that I'd have to cash in my meager savings from babysitting jobs, birthday gifts, and household chores just to afford their manicures. But *they* couldn't pay.

"So, we'll see you Saturday afternoon at two o'clock, okay?" I asked. "Thanks!"

"No, thank *you*," Cassidy said sweetly.

The syrupy tone to her voice made me a little nauseous. If she hadn't been such a good friend to me not that long ago, it would have made no sense at all.

"Wait—Madison!" Cassidy suddenly called as I started to walk away.

"Yeah?" I paused.

"You know that day, when you got your hair cut. We did this online thing, and it was really stupid, and I'm totally sorry about it," said Cassidy. "It was so immature. I mean, I bet you didn't even *see* it, but if you did see it—"

"I saw it," I said calmly.

"Sorry," Cassidy and Alexis said at the same time.

"It's, uh, okay. I mean, thanks. I guess."

I walked back to the T-shirt table, kind of in a daze.

"Did they say yes?" Olivia asked, looking up at me.

I nodded. "They're pretty excited about the idea of a free manicure."

"Thank goodness." Taylor sighed. "I thought for sure they were going to turn us down."

"Me too," Olivia said. "In fact, if they show up and this actually works, I'll be totally shocked."

"Agreed. It's a juvenile and misguided plan, just like your idea to get rid of them in the first place with that stupid ceremony," Taylor added. She turned to Olivia. "What were we thinking when we agreed to go along with Madison?"

The way she was glaring at me, and the way her words stung, it was almost as if she'd just punched me in the jaw. We'd been friends for so long, and now she was sitting there, criticizing every single thing about me.

"Well, at least I did *something*," I said. "At least I tried."

"Well, maybe don't try so hard next time," Taylor said.

I glanced around the cafeteria, angry tears filling my eyes, tears that I didn't want Taylor or Olivia or anyone else in the room to see. "You know, if that's how you feel, you don't have to come Saturday. Neither of you have to come. I'm the one who started all this, and I can stop it on my own."

"Oh, we'll be there," Olivia said. "We have to make sure you don't screw up."

Where was all this coming from? Since when did I screw up everything? "You know what? Sometimes, I don't even know why we're friends," I said.

Taylor folded her arms across her chest. "Sometimes, neither do I."

"Then we definitely don't have to *stay* friends!" I said.

I walked out of the cafeteria, tossing the burned cupcake into the trash on my way.

We'd never had a fight as bad as this—ever. Everyday teasing or giving each other a hard time—that was one thing. But now, all of a sudden, it seemed everyone had turned on me. Instead of standing up to the mean girls together, we'd split apart, and I'd ended up alone.

Maybe I'd lost the mean girls—or a little of their meanness—but I'd lost my friends, too.

What if we went ahead with the meanicure party and it *didn't* work? *Then* where would I be? It'd be five mean girls against me. I didn't want to think about those odds. Or had I turned into one, too?

We were halfway through dinner—Chinese takeout—which I wasn't eating, when Mom reached over and put her hand on my arm. "You're so quiet. What's wrong? What happened?"

Sometimes when I try to hide things from her, she notices them even more. I like that and I hate it at the same time.

"She got those photos back from Halloween," Parker said.

"Quiet," Mom warned him.

"She realized that what she thought was a fake wart was actually a real wart, which means her nose is that warty all the time," he went on.

"Knock it off. I need to hear from Madison, not you," Mom said sternly.

"Fine." Parker dished more fried rice onto his plate, making a mound the size of a football. He always insists on using chopsticks, even though he can hardly pick up a shrimp with them, never mind endless grains of rice. I wouldn't mind, but I have to stay at the table until he's done, too—it's a family rule. I have better things to do with my life than watch him try to catch sticky rice with a chopstick.

At least, I used to.

"Madison. Spill," Mom told me as I stacked baby corn with my fork to make a miniature cabin. It's amazing the projects you can start when you're stalling at the dinner table.

"We sort of had a fight."

"Who?"

"My . . ." I was going to say "friends" but it didn't seem accurate. "Olivia. And Taylor. They totally took shots at me this afternoon."

"Seriously? They hit you?" asked Parker.

"Not shots like that. Just verbal shots," I explained.

"Why would Olivia and Taylor do that to you?" Mom took a sip of water, so calm that I found myself becoming irritated. I wanted her to grab the phone and call somebody, make things right. Or I wanted her to scream a little and be outraged. She could wave that magic Mom wand she used to have and make every-thing stop hurting with a Disney Band-Aid.

139

"That's the thing. I don't know why they did, exactly," I said. "I mean, I kind of know. But . . ."

"Madison, you're not making sense. Tell me what happened."

I shook my head. "I can't tell you."

"Sure you can."

"No."

Mom looked exasperated. "If you refuse to give me any more information than that, then I can't help you. But I'm sure that any argument you had isn't permanent. I bet it'll have blown over by the time you go to bed tonight."

I narrowed my eyes. How could she talk about my life like it was a weather front? "I don't think so," I said.

She went on, offering more unhelpful advice. "Sometimes we don't know why people say what they do. Maybe they're just having a bad day, but they take it out on us. All you can do is ride out the storm."

"Mom, I'm sick of your weather metaphors! They don't help!"

She looked startled. "Maybe not now, I know. But—"

"No, you don't know. You don't understand." I pushed back my chair, leaving my uneaten dinner on the table, and ran for the stairs. I slammed the door to my room and flopped onto the bed, head on hands, staring out at the ocean. There was a gleam of moonlight on the water.

Maybe that's a sign, I thought. For a second I had this

brief glimmer of hope. Maybe someone had already apologized. Maybe something good was about to happen. I jumped up to check my computer.

Nope. No e-mail. Nothing.

Parker opened the door a crack and poked his head in. So much for hope. (Not to mention privacy.)

"You know what?" he asked. "Don't sweat it. They'll get over it, and so will you."

"Right," I said. "What makes you think that?"

"You've been friends forever, why would you *stop* now?" he said. "People don't just stop being friends."

"Cassidy and I stopped," I reminded him.

"Oh. Yeah. Well, uh . . ."

Usually I'm thrilled when Parker is speechless. This time . . . not so much.

That night, I couldn't sleep. I tried reading a book; I watched a movie; I even read my math book, cover to cover. I couldn't stop worrying about the manicures. Would they work? Would my friends become my friends again? Would we all stop being so mean, or would just some of us change back? What if it *didn't* work, and we were stuck this way forever? I couldn't let that happen.

Finally I got up, pulled on my robe, and went downstairs. First I sorted through Mom's boxes of samples in the basement, putting together custom gift bags—not just for the original mean girls but for Olivia and Taylor, too.

Maybe sample sizes weren't enough, I thought as I filled the small canvas bags Mom always kept on hand for gifts to prospective clients. Maybe we needed the quart sizes. Or the gallon ones.

After those were done and labeled, I went up to the kitchen. I found a box of cake mix, but first I quickly made a batch of Rice Krispies Treats with chocolate chips.

This is going to work, I told myself as I slid the angel food cake pan into the oven at midnight. *This has to work.*

Chapter 18

"Poinsettia, do you think they'll show?" I paced back and forth by the front window of Combing Attractions on Saturday afternoon.

"Oh, I don't know," she said casually, looking up from the front counter and sounding unconcerned. "I bet they will."

"But it's five to two," I said. "And no one's here yet!" I was having flashbacks to our Endangered Animals Club meeting. I couldn't take being so unpopular all over again—especially since two of the people coming were supposed to be my best friends.

"So tell me again, since we have time," Poinsettia prompted, "who was closest friends with whom?" She lazily stirred a packet of sugar into a cup of coffee. How could she be so relaxed when so much was on the line? Then again, it wasn't *her* life that was out of control and nearly ruined.

"How many times do I have to go over this?" I asked.

"Once more," she said, "so I know how to help."

"Right. Right. Sorry," I told her. She was helping. A lot.

She was doing this as a special favor, and even though I was paying her for the manicures, she was going above and beyond her beauty consultant title.

We discussed things and decided that she would begin with me and Cassidy, but make it look casual. "You'll set the tone," Poinsettia said.

"How?" I asked. "And how will two of us go at the same time?" I still didn't understand how we were going to pull this off.

"I told you, I work in phases. Really, it's not a big deal. If things start moving too slowly, I'll get someone to help me," she said. "Anyway, what I'll do with you and Cassidy is give you an opening in the conversation. When I do, take it, run with it. Don't look back."

She made it sound like the torch for the Olympic Games. I couldn't handle that much pressure.

Finally, just when I thought I couldn't take it any longer, I spotted Taylor and Olivia walking up to the shop.

I hurried into a chair, flipped open a magazine, and tried to act casual. I glanced up as they walked in, ducking under the giant comb hanging from the doorway.

"Hey," Taylor said. She slid into the chair next to mine.

"Oh. Hey," I replied back awkwardly.

We might as well have been complete strangers.

"And you are?" Poinsettia prompted from the desk.

"I'm Olivia. And that's Taylor." Olivia checked out

the waiting area and peered around the rest of the salon, while Poinsettia checked them off her list. I kept my nose in the magazine. I wished I'd picked up something besides the most recent issue of *Fortune Tellers Monthly*.

After a minute, Taylor went up to the desk and asked, "Excuse me? Could you turn down the A/C? It's freezing in here." She was wearing a tank top, a pair of black yoga pants, and flip-flops.

Poinsettia looked up and said, "The air conditioning's not on."

"Oh."

"Perhaps you shouldn't have dressed as if it were still July. Now, please excuse me while I go make sure the room is set up and ready for all of you," Poinsettia said.

"Well, can you turn up the heat back there?" asked Taylor. "My hands are ice cold."

Poinsettia arched one of her eyebrows, and Taylor quickly added, "Please, if you don't mind, that'd be really nice," and smiled. She glanced at me, her smile vanishing as she sat down again.

Wow. I thought I'd never have the power to make someone stop *smiling*. Before I could think of anything witty or worthwhile to say, though, the door opened and Cassidy, Alexis, and Kayley walked into the salon.

"This place is so cute!" Cassidy nearly hit her head on one of the big dangling combs. "I've never even heard of anyone who's gone here. Well, except you. You're so, like, *adventurous,* with your hair and everything." She looked at me with a small smile.

"Thanks so much for inviting us," Alexis said as she shrugged off her red wool peacoat, which perfectly matched her red leather boots. "Hey, cool hanger," she added, noticing the coat hangers made of big combs.

"I'm really grateful, but I'm worried this is going to kill me." Kayley slid her tiny black purse off her shoulder, then struggled to pull her down vest over her bandaged wrist. "I can't even straighten my wrist, so how will I get a manicure?"

"You could get a pedicure instead," Taylor said.

"No, she couldn't," I said. That would ruin the whole concept, in my view. It was a meanicure, not a pedicure. Plus, pedicures cost a lot more money. I was already broke. "It's manicures only."

"Who died and made you in charge?" Taylor asked.

Um . . . it was my idea? I wanted to say. *And when it's your idea, you're sort of in charge, like it or not.* I was definitely on the "not" side. "Okay . . . then get a pedicure," I said. "What do I care? But you'll have to find out how much it costs, because we only paid for manicures."

"I'll just ask her if she can be really, really careful. I'm sure it'll be fine." Kayley smiled. She was being so agreeable that it was weird.

We walked through the curtains made of dangling nail polish bottles clinking gently against one another, straight into Paint-on Place.

146

Poinsettia was waiting for us. "Girls, help yourselves to treats, courtesy of your hosts."

Host, I thought. Singular.

A long black table, which had pyramids of polish displays at one end, was covered with the snacks: chocolate-chip Rice Krispies Treats, angel food cake, and bowls of Honey Nut Cheerios. I'd also brought cans of soda, flavored bottled water, and juice. I was trying to cure everybody with sweetness. I'd nearly keeled over on my bike from carrying so much stuff—both in a backpack and also in a milk crate tied with bungee cords to the rack over my back tire (I'd copied the way my mom set up her bike when she pedaled to the grocery store).

"Wow. For us? You guys did a lot." Cassidy seemed shocked.

"Yeah, we did," said Olivia, looking a little stunned herself.

I glared at her. She'd done nothing. I had done everything. As usual. "I made these, too." I pointed to the gift bags on the table, each one labeled with a girl's name.

"Whoa. I *love* gift bags." Alexis peered into the tiny canvas tote. "And free products!"

"I still don't understand why we're here, exactly," said Kayley. "I mean, why would you want to do all this for us?"

"Enough chatting." Poinsettia clapped her hands together. "Pick your colors, everybody, pick your colors. Let's get this show on the road."

"Seriously, though. Why *did* you guys want to do this for us?" Cassidy asked me while we contemplated which of the thirty shades we wanted.

While I stalled, trying to think of a good answer, I considered green for my nails, then purple, then black. What would be the best color for a meanicure? A rainbow? "Well, see . . . things have been kind of, you know, strained," I finally said. "Since Halloween. I wanted to patch things up before the holidays."

"What's to patch up? We get along fine," said Cassidy, "most of the time." She picked up the same silver metallic shade that I'd just started admiring. Maybe we didn't have as much in common anymore, but there were still a *few* things.

"Yeah. Well, but I was pretty awful that night," I said. "Egging you. And other things. And I just really like this place, so I wanted to share it."

"Who's going to go first? I think I'll start with you two." Poinsettia pointed at me and Cassidy.

"Why two at a time?" asked Cassidy.

"I like to keep things moving," Poinsettia replied. "The rest of you enjoy the snacks."

Cassidy and I sat in the red leather chairs and Poinsettia got to work. First we had to soak our nails in bowls of a strong-smelling liquid that reminded me of my mom's Pine Tree Protein Rinse.

Poinsettia told us the liquid had special powers to relax us and heal our cuticles. Then she began to file and shape Cassidy's nails, while I sat there, feeling like I was supposed to say something very important at this point, but not knowing what. The minutes were ticking by.

Nobody was really talking yet. I'd created this opportunity, and if I didn't act soon, I'd be wasting it.

"You really have bitten your nails to shreds," Poinsettia commented.

Cassidy sighed. "It's a bad habit, I know. My mom never stops telling me that," she said.

"What makes you do it?" I asked. "You never used to bite your nails."

Poinsettia coughed. Then she cleared her throat. Suddenly it dawned on me. She was trying to tell me: this was it. My opening. I should take it and run.

"So, is there a reason? I mean . . . what's going on?" I asked.

"Oh, my life's been a little, um, stressful." Cassidy smiled.

"I can put some artificial tips on you," Poinsettia said. "Give you a little added length—nothing tacky. I'll use short ones so they look natural."

"I don't know." Cassidy looked at her nails, and then looked over at mine. "How much does that even cost?"

"Don't worry about that. Today's a special group deal," said Poinsettia.

I smiled at her, grateful for the generous offer. "If you want, Cassidy, I'll do it with you," I said. "I mean, I'll go artificial, too. How about that?"

She thought it over for a second, then said, "Sure. Okay."

I took a deep breath. If I didn't start talking to her, I'd waste the opportunity I'd worked so hard to create. "So. What's been so, um, stressful?" I asked. "Besides what I know about already." *Which I may be somewhat responsible for, which means I'm also responsible for your short fingernails.*

"Do you want the long version or the short version?" Cassidy said.

"Whichever," I said. "We're going to be here a while, right?"

"If your nails are anywhere as bad as hers, then yes," Poinsettia said. "What is *with* you girls? Can't you just chew gum when you're upset?" She expertly worked a nail buffer over Cassidy's nails, smoothing them out and preparing them for the artificial tips and polish.

"Well, first off, did I tell you I tried out for cheer captain? What a nightmare. Needless to say, I did not get chosen. They totally made fun of me. Of course, they waited until I wrote my mission statement, and gave a speech about what I'd do, and choreographed an entire new cheer. Then they told me they'd never choose a seventh grader. And acted like 'who do you think you are?'"

"That wasn't fair," I said. "Why didn't they announce up front that it was only open to eighth graders?"

"I don't know," she said. "So they could laugh at me?"

"I can't believe the other girls were rude to you like that," I said. "That's terrible." But all I could think was, *You still hang out with them, after that? Why?* "Like someone in eighth grade is so much older and better than someone in seventh?"

Cassidy nodded. "See? *You* understand. You get it. I try to tell other people and they're clueless." She glanced over at me and smiled.

"So, what else is going on? I mean, how's your year going? I've hardly talked to you." *Because you haven't let me.* "Is there anything else bugging you?" I asked.

"Oh, yeah. I'm getting a D in English. I can't write essays the way I'm supposedly . . . supposed to." She laughed. "You know how to do all that. You're the writer, not me."

I remembered helping her with her essays back in sixth grade. "You'll get the hang of it."

"Or not," she said.

"Whenever I'm bored by an assignment, I can't write at all," I said. "Maybe you just need a subject that interests you more."

"And maybe I need a tutor. My mom wants me to go to that tutor place at the mall. You know that little place right next to the arcade, with the really ugly sign? Let Us Teach You? Can you imagine walking out of there and running into someone from school? I mean, can you even imagine how embarrassing that would be? I'd rather get a D."

"You could always wear a hat. A disguise," I said.

She burst out laughing. "Like that time we were at Macy's, and Hunter and his friends came in?"

My face felt like it was turning bright red at the memory. We'd been dragged to Macy's to shop for bras with our mothers, and a saleslady was heading toward me with a measuring tape when Cassidy spotted the boys weaving our way. The bra department had the worst location ever—right near one of the mall doors, so everyone passed by while you were holding really embarrassing items and your moms were talking about how you needed "good support."

Fortunately lingerie was also right next to the accessories department, and by the time they walked past we were wearing hats and holding umbrellas over our heads.

I burst out laughing, too, and Cassidy and I laughed and laughed, causing Poinsettia to stop for a second, not mad at all, just with a smile on her face.

But others apparently didn't share the joy. Alexis stomped over in her red high-heeled boots, narrowing her eyes at me and Cassidy. "Is everything okay over here?" she asked.

"Good support!" Cassidy said through her laughter, which made me laugh even harder.

"'You girls are ridiculous!'" I said in between giggles, quoting what both our moms had said at the time. "'Ridiculous!'"

Alexis put her hands on her hips. "What's going on?"

"Nothing, none of your business, okay? Chill out."
Cassidy glanced at me and rolled her eyes.

"Fine. But you sound crazy," Alexis said before she
walked back to the sofa.

"Oh, we are," I said. I looked down at my nails,
feeling happy but also confused. Cassidy and I hadn't
connected like this in months. Why couldn't we
always? Was the strong smell of nail polish going to
our heads?

"So. I'm, you know. *Still* sorry about Halloween and
the egging stuff," I said.

"Don't worry about it. I actually enjoyed watching
my stepdad scraping it off the doorway," Cassidy said.

"Oh?" I asked.

"Yes. He hates eggs." She laughed. "And he's such
a neat freak. Everything has to be a certain way. And
he keeps changing stuff around the house. Constantly.
He got us new furniture, and he made the living room
into the dining room, and my old room is now the guest
room so I have the attic to myself but I don't like the
attic, and he turned an old closet into a 'nook,' whatever
that is."

"I thought it looked different! So he's Mr. Home
Improvement?" I asked.

"Our house is a construction zone. I can't hear
myself think," Cassidy complained.

"Reminds me of an ex of mine," Poinsettia chimed in.
"So busy fixing things he didn't notice everything else
that was breaking."

"Deep." Cassidy looked at me and rolled her eyes.

I smiled, then cracked up laughing with her. But then I thought about it. I hadn't known things with Cassidy had gotten harder since her mom remarried. I guess I'd thought they'd be easier. Was that why we drifted apart? Because we both didn't have single moms in common anymore?

But we hadn't *drifted*. She'd slammed the door in my face. She'd stepped into some new life, and after I dropped out of cheer because I realized I didn't love it anymore and was only going through the motions, literally, Cassidy had ditched me and hadn't looked back.

"Hey, all I'm saying is, sometimes people don't pay attention like they should." Poinsettia looked closely at Cassidy. "Like you and your nails. Get some sleep. Take more calcium and vitamin B."

Cassidy turned to me again. "How do you deal with it? I mean, what about that guy your mom's seeing. You like him?" she asked.

"Sure. David's okay," I said. "He's funny, he's nice. He's good to my mom."

"Are they going to get married?" asked Cassidy.

"What?" I shook my head. "*My* mom? No, Mom will never get married."

"Why not? Mine did. I never thought she would, remember?"

"Hm. I hadn't thought about it." It's weird when someone's known you longer than anyone. They're kind of like cousins. I'd sort of forgotten about Cassidy's mom's wedding, back when we were in fifth grade. Cassidy had worn a dress she positively hated. I pictured myself in an equally hideous dress. "Don't stress me out!" I said. "They've been dating for a couple of years. If they were going to get married, wouldn't they have done that by now?"

Cassidy laughed. "Not necessarily."

I felt this worry spot start to grow inside me. Mom . . . married? To David? The more I thought about it, the bigger the spot grew.

Thankfully, Cassidy seemed to sense I was floundering and changed the subject. "You know what? Maybe you're not as into cheerleading as you used to be, but you were good, plus you kept me and Alexis from fighting. Don't you ever think about coming back?"

That was the last thing I expected her to say. "Me? Um, not really."

"But how could you just quit on us?"

I didn't know what to say without hurting her feelings. I guess I had already hurt them. Just because I didn't feel like a cheer person anymore didn't mean I'd quit on *Cassidy*. Ms. Throgfeld had pulled me aside at the end of sixth grade and told me if my heart wasn't in it a hundred percent, I shouldn't bother. And honestly? My heart wasn't in it even fifty percent. "I just . . . lost a step, or something. I felt like I was being phony."

She stared at me as if she had no idea what I could possibly be talking about. We had a lot in common still, but we had also grown apart. "You should think about coming back," Cassidy said. "I mean, if you want to add to your coolness factor."

"Coolness factor?" I said.

"Exactly."

"Right, I'll think about it," I said. "And you know, if your stepdad is ever driving you really crazy, come to our house. It's usually pretty quiet. We have the quietness factor."

"Yeah, but your mom will want to color my hair with some experimental stuff," said Cassidy. "I can't take that risk."

"No doubt." I exchanged a look with Poinsettia. "Thankfully that's all over for me."

"Why? Who's your mom?" asked Poinsettia.

Cassidy gasped. "You don't *know*?"

"Nope."

"Nik's Organix. She's the one who created it," said Cassidy.

"Oh, yeah?" asked Poinsettia. "That hippie stuff made out of honey and aloe and oregano?"

I laughed. "It's not oregano."

"No?"

"No, it's seaweed," I said.

Poinsettia arched an eyebrow. "Like that's better? Okay, all done here, girls. What do you think?"

Cassidy and I admired our new, longer, silver metallic nails. "Beautiful," said Cassidy. "I can't wait to show everyone at school!"

We moved to the sofa while Taylor and Kayley started picking nail polish colors with Poinsettia. Kayley decided to get a pedicure after all, and started soaking her feet; Taylor chose to stick with the manicure. I overheard Kayley talking with Taylor about the stress of having so many new siblings in her blended family, and how the only place she could be free was in the gym. Taylor was nodding and agreeing a lot. Poinsettia started applying polish to Taylor's nails— she and Kayley had both chosen a deep blood-red color.

Beside me, Olivia and Alexis were talking and munching on the Rice Krispies Treats, while they leafed through hairstyle magazines, laughing. *So far, so good*, I thought. Maybe the three of *us*, Olivia, Taylor, and I weren't on speaking terms, but if everyone else was—

Suddenly Alexis sat forward in her seat. "Why are you asking me so many questions? What are you up to?" she asked in a loud voice.

"N-nothing," Olivia said.

"You're going to use this information against me or something. Aren't you?" Alexis demanded.

"What? No!" Olivia shook her head. "Don't be so paranoid. I'm just trying to catch up after all this time."

"All what time? What are you talking about? I see you every day, almost," said Alexis. "So what's with the nosy, third-degree stuff?"

"She's right," said Cassidy. "You guys are asking way too many questions." She stared at me, looking genuinely hurt. "Was that why you were being so nice to me? Because this is a setup?"

"No!" I said.

"I don't believe you. You know, I should have known you guys were up to something. You never just invite us anywhere anymore," she said.

"*Us?* What about *you*?" I said. "You only talk to us when you want to trick us or insult us!"

"As if." Cassidy got to her feet, waving her nails in the air to dry them. "Come on, guys. We're out of here. Let's get our coats."

"But—" Kayley looked up, her feet still soaking in the pedicure bath.

"Now," said Cassidy, tugging at her sleeve.

Kayley got to her feet, and slipped on the paper flip-flops that she was supposed to wear after her pedicure.

And just like that, they whisked through the dangling, clinking nail polish bottles and were gone.

"Well, what are you waiting for?" said Poinsettia. "Go after them!"

Chapter 19

The table by the sofa was covered with abandoned gift bags and plates of half-eaten treats. The inside of the angel's food cake was so jagged that it looked like it had been sliced—no, sawed—with a nail file.

"I *told* you this wouldn't work," Olivia muttered under her breath, straightening the magazines. "I *told* you it was a dumb plan."

Taylor turned to Olivia, hands on her hips. "You know what? The plan was working. But I should have known you couldn't pull this off. I should have known you'd—"

"This isn't the time to point fingers," I said. "It's like Poinsettia said. Let's go find them already!" I headed right for the door. I knew there were only a couple of places they could have gone without a car, and the quicker we moved, the better. We dashed down the red carpet to the sidewalk.

"Look." Taylor pointed at the sidewalk. "Kayley left footprints."

"Man. No socks, and wet feet? She must be freezing," I said.

"Could those footprints be any smaller?" asked Olivia. "They're like a child's feet."

"So we're small—sue us." Taylor hustled alongside me, in a half walk, half jog, following the footprints. She was waving her three freshly painted nails in the air to dry them.

All of a sudden, the footprints ended. Nothing on the sidewalk. No clue.

"Okay . . . ," Olivia said. "Now what? Did someone start carrying her?"

"I know—we can look for crumbs," said Olivia. "Alexis was eating a Rice Krispies Treat when she ran out."

The three of us stared at the ground, desperate for cereal crumbs. We were like three pathetic birds on the lookout for a morsel.

"This Nancy Drew detective thing is lame. Why not just try the coffee shop?" I asked. "I mean, where else are they going to go?"

"I guess," said Taylor, like she was only agreeing in order to humor me. Seriously, where else would they go? Roadrunner Records? Eastern Cycle Supply? Hal's Hearing Aids?

We jogged the half block to Bean-a-While, our town's ancient coffee shop that is usually full of aging hippies, even older and more hippie-ish than my mom, and smells vaguely of patchouli, herbal tea, and espresso.

As I stopped outside the entrance, I heard a crunch under my foot and found a fake silver nail tip stuck to the bottom of my shoe. "See?" I said. "They're in here."

"Great!" Taylor reached for the door, but I put my hand on her arm.

"Wait, stop!" I said.

"Why? Do you see them somewhere else?" asked Olivia.

"No. It's just . . . we haven't talked about this yet. What are we even going to *say*?"

They both stared at me as if I was ruining the thrill of the chase. But really, we had to decide on something before we just marched in. Cassidy was right; this *was* a setup. We had done it with good intentions, but would they care?

"Oh. Hadn't thought about that yet," said Olivia.

"Well, I have," I said. And I knew that to make this right, we'd have to team up. I wasn't sure if we knew how to team up anymore. Would everyone just turn on me when things got difficult. I wasn't up for any more Madison-bashing. "And before we go inside to try to fix things with the Original Mean Girls, I think we need to fix things between us first." I knew I sounded braver than I felt inside.

"Fix what?" Olivia asked.

Taylor tucked her hands under her armpits. "I'm freezing. Can we talk about this later?"

I shook my head. "No. Listen, if we're being fake, then there's no way we'll convince them to come back with us." I took a deep breath. "We're only pretending to be friends right now. We're not really being friends."

"We're not?" asked Olivia.

"Not to me," I said. My voice came out a lot weaker than I wanted it to. But I was still hurt.

"Madison's right." Taylor stepped a little closer to me. "We've really been acting like jerks to you lately, Madison. And I'm sorry."

"Me too," said Olivia.

"I know I haven't exactly been nice, either," I said.

"Maybe not, but we shouldn't have blamed you for everything," Taylor said. "We're all in this together. Right?"

"Right," agreed Olivia. "And we've all made mistakes."

"Big ones. So let's agree that we're not going to act like that toward each other ever again," Taylor declared. "Okay? Because when we do, we're not being friends. We're being mean girls. And not even original ones. We're like copy mean girls, which is weak."

We put our hands together, stacked on top of each other. One of my fake nails clattered onto the sidewalk, and I stomped on it, so now it was stuck to the underside of my other shoe. As I walked, I sounded like a tap dancer. But the pack was back together. That meant I could handle almost anything.

"So when we go in there, we'll just be honest and tell them everything," I said. "Right?"

"Um, how about almost everything?" Olivia suggested. "Let's leave out the part about the fire and exploding pom-poms. We'll be mostly honest."

Snow suddenly started to fall, thick, fat flakes swirling around us. We had these furious snow squalls from time to time in the spring and fall—they didn't usually last long. They were temporary, kind of like fights between friends.

"So what are we going to say?" asked Taylor. "That we did this because we want to be friends with them again?"

I thought about it for a minute. I didn't want to be friends with anyone who was mean to me most of the time. "No . . . I guess we don't want that, exactly. That'd be phony. Let's just tell them that we want to *not* be enemies."

"Great. Let's go inside!" Taylor threw open the door and we raced in, brushing snowflakes off our shoulders and hair.

Cassidy, Kayley, and Alexis were huddled in a booth by the side window. Between them, they had one can of soda, and three paper cups. They looked miserable. When they looked over and saw us standing next to their table, they didn't smile.

"It's snowing," I said. "Can you believe it?"

"Thrilling," Alexis commented dryly. Kayley glared at us. Cassidy wouldn't make eye contact.

"I bet it'll stop soon," said Taylor. "One of those snow squall–type things. Um, can you guys slide in and make room?"

"*No,*" said Kayley.

"Fine." I shrugged.

"Not until you explain what's going on," said Cassidy, eyes narrowed.

"We're going to explain everything!" I said. "Just give us a second."

Us. I looked to Olivia and Taylor for help, but for some reason they were avoiding eye contact with me, too. *Sure, leave the hard part to me!* I thought. But then I realized: *I'm the one who got us into this . . . I can get us out.*

"The reason we invited you and wanted to talk was really simple. We just wanted to reconnect," I said.

Cassidy wrinkled her nose. "Reconnect *what*?" she asked. "You make it sound like we're lightbulbs."

"Extension cords, actually," Taylor said.

I glared at her. Was that helping? That was *not* helping.

Thankfully, Olivia chimed in. "You know, reconnect with you guys, because we drifted apart. Like a sailboat going off course."

"We felt like we just were kind of, um, on the wrong foot. Feet." Taylor laughed nervously. "You know, like every time we talked to you, or didn't talk to you . . . anyway, it wasn't good. We thought maybe if we all just got together and hung out, we could make things better."

"Why do things need to be better?" asked Cassidy.

She really had no clue. This was so interesting. And so awful, too.

Kayley coughed. "We don't trust anyone who's that nice to us. Because why would you be that nice without wanting something in return?"

"That's just *weird*," I said. "People can be nice for no reason."

"Not usually," Cassidy said. "Ever notice how when your parents are really nice, it's fake? Like, they only act that way long enough for you to agree that you have to do your homework and you don't care about having the newest iPod. Which is a total lie. They distract you with all this niceness."

"But we weren't trying to trick you or get information to use against you," I said. "We have completely innocent intentions." Complicated, maybe, but innocent. *I thought, or, actually, Poinsettia thought that maybe if we found out why you were being so mean to us all the time, we could stop being mean ourselves, undo the ceremony, and then maybe we could keep it all from happening again.* But I couldn't say that to them. "We really just wanted to kind of make things right."

Cassidy looked at me like she still wasn't sure whether to believe me or not. That made sense. She'd known me longer than anyone; she could probably tell when I wasn't being totally honest. "You know what? Let's get out of here." She suddenly got to her feet. "I left my wallet in my coat, which is back at the salon, so we only had enough change in our pockets to buy one root beer. Do you think you guys could go get our coats, and bring them back here for us? It's freezing out there."

"No. We don't even have *our* coats," Taylor said.

"Well, speaking of shoes, do you think one of you

could carry Kayley? She's getting frostbite," Cassidy said.

"Sure," said Olivia. "I can do it. I have to carry my little sister all the ti—" She stopped as she realized Kayley was glaring at her. "Of course," she added, "Laney's much smaller than you. *Much*."

"So, will you guys come back and finish the me—the manicure?" I asked. "It's all been paid for, plus we have tons of snacks, and then there are the gift bags. It would be a shame to waste everything."

"I guess," Cassidy said, holding out her hands to admire them again, even with the one missing artificial nail. "She really is good."

"Cassidy? I wasn't being phony when we were talking. I meant every word," I told her as I followed her to the door. "You can always still just show up at my house, any time you want."

"Yeah, right. Why would I want to?" she replied.

Whatever Cassidy had been willing to share with me before, she was done sharing now. It was like a little window had been opened but now it was closed again.

But now I knew a little bit of what was going on with her. It didn't explain why she was mean to me sometimes, but it did explain what she had to deal with.

"You know what? It's impossible to make a dramatic exit around here," she said now. "You forget your coat, your wallet—"

"And your shoes," added Kayley.

"And then it starts snowing." Cassidy shook her head.

"It's Payneston." I opened the door and got a wet, fat flake of snow right in my eye. "What do you expect?"

About an hour and a half later, we all had nice, colorful nails (Poinsettia had fixed our broken ones), and people were being a little bit more real with each other. It was like we were in a mean-free zone; they weren't being horrible, and neither were we.

Everyone gathered around the gift bags on the table as I packed the leftover snacks into my backpack, deciding to leave all the sodas and waters behind for whoever wanted them. I couldn't let the day end without some kind of official statement, some attempt to finally put this behind us. But I had no idea how to do it. I wasn't ready for this moment.

And inside, I was freaking out about it. What if getting your nails done and just catching up *wasn't* enough? Would I have to swallow fire or make up a recipe for angeled eggs?

Dejected, I picked up my backpack and followed the group to the door, stopping by the front desk to thank Poinsettia. "Help?" I mouthed silently.

She was already way ahead of me. "I like to keep a record of manicure parties. It helps market them to other clients." She handed out a printed photo collage to everyone. I hadn't noticed her with a camera, but she'd taken separate photos of us getting our manicures, and the collage showed all of us laughing and talking and having a good time.

"When did you take these?" Olivia asked.

"Did I forget to mention that I have special powers?" Poinsettia smiled. "Not to mention co-workers. Now you'll have a memento so you can remember what it's like to just hang out and be friends."

"We don't need a record," Cassidy scoffed, but I noticed her smile as she looked at the photos.

"Yeah, we'll remember," Alexis insisted.

Really? I thought. *We'll see.*

"But, uh, do you sell the nail polish, too?" Cassidy asked. "I'd like to take some home, because I'll probably need a new coat next week."

Everyone lined up to purchase a bottle of nail polish.

"Thanks so much. And can I make an appointment for a haircut next week?" Olivia asked Poinsettia when it was her turn.

"It's about time. Shaggy much?" commented Alexis.

Cassidy and Kayley held their hands over their mouths and snickered.

"It's amazing how often people forget to make appointments. Even you two." Poinsettia applied a fresh coat of bright red lipstick. "Now, if you'll excuse me . . ." She gestured to her next client.

We gathered by the coat rack. "So," I said.

"So." Cassidy grabbed her coat from the hanger and slipped it on.

"Nice jacket," I said to her.

She didn't thank me.

As we stepped out onto the sidewalk, we looked at each other like we hadn't just spent the afternoon together, hanging out and having fun. Like that wasn't allowed. Like we weren't all holding gift bags from the same event. Immediately we separated into our normal pattern: their three and our three. It was like that was the only way we knew how.

"We have to go," said Cassidy.

Kayley nodded, adjusting her tiny purse on her tiny shoulder. "Yeah, we're meeting someone at the movies."

"What movie?" asked Olivia.

"Um . . ." Kayley tapped her index finger against her cheek. "I don't know. Did we decide yet?"

Alexis shook her head. "No. We didn't."

"Definitely not," added Cassidy.

I couldn't help rolling my eyes. What did they think, that we were going to show up at the movies? That we'd follow them around like puppies? Meanicure or not, they were back to their usual selves. Did it matter that I'd sort of reconnected with Cassidy, and my friends had gotten in touch with their former friends a little bit, too?

"See you around?" I asked, turning to walk in the opposite direction.

"Right. I'll see you!" Cassidy called over her shoulder.

And that was that. We went our way, and they went theirs.

"We have plans, too!" Olivia shouted after them. "Big plans!"

"We do?" I asked in a soft voice, so they couldn't overhear.

"No, but if they're going to act like *that* again, like they're the only ones who can make plans, I am not going to just stand here and take it," said Olivia. "Anyway. Laney has a soccer game at the park near here. Want to go watch?" she asked.

Taylor and I looked at each other, considering it. "Sure, why not?" I said. "I don't have anywhere else I have to be."

"Me neither," said Taylor.

I started to unlock my bike, then stopped. "You know what? Since you guys are walking, I'll walk, too. I'll just come back later for my bike," I said.

"Are you sure?" asked Olivia.

"Definitely," I said.

We started down the sidewalk together, walking side by side. Then we put our arms around each other's shoulders and walked, three across, laughing, giggling, pushing, and leaning our way across town through the snow, which had almost stopped.

The best thing about the meanicure was that if the mean girls were back to being themselves, that meant we could go back to being ourselves, too.

Friends.

The kind of friends you could skip down the street with, side by side, arms linked, not worrying at all about your coolness factor, because you didn't care what anyone else thought, as long as you had each other.

Chapter 20

"Good morning, everyone. I'm Olivia Salinas with this morning's update."

I held my breath as I sat in homeroom, watching the television screen mounted to the wall. I crossed my fingers. I drummed my new, shiny silver fingernails against my desk.

"You feeling all right, Madison?" Ms. Thibault asked, pausing beside me.

"Sure. Just, uh, wondering what Olivia will say," I said. That, and Poinsettia had told me that tapping my fingers on hard surfaces might help my nails grow.

Ms. Thibault laughed and put her hand on my shoulder. "I think we *all* are, at this point."

Everyone who's listening, that is, I thought.

Olivia looked into the camera and smiled. "What a weekend. Did everyone have as good a weekend as I did? I hope so.

"Okay, first things first, the schedule for the upcoming week is as follows," she began. "It's our last full week before Thanksgiving break, so there's a lot to pack in." She ran through the list of events, games, and club meetings. She didn't add anything extra. Everything seemed to go according to plan; she read the student council news, which wasn't much, and she didn't insult anyone.

As she wrapped up, she said, "On a personal note, this reporter would like to apologize for being rude. I'm sorry that I've said some things I regret. Please, please join us this afternoon to save the endangered animals. We're off to a great start. You've seen the T-shirts. We're temporarily out of stock on those, but we're planning the Christmas dance-a-thon. It's never too early to start your pledge sheet. So please come! Have a great day, Panthers!" She smiled genuinely at the camera before the screen went dark.

"Well? Did she do all right?" Ms. Thibault asked me.

"Bo—ring," said Justin.

Bethany patted her mouth. "Yawn City."

"Um, I think that's probably the last time we'll be hearing from Olivia for a while," I said.

"Too bad," said Bethany. "At least she made things interesting and unpredictable for a while."

"Don't forget Madison," said Justin. "The rrrrain in Mmmmaine stays mmmmainly—"

"Don't remind me!" I put my hands over my ears. *"Please!"*

The rest of the day seemed to continue the shift back to normal. At lunch, Taylor was carrying Kayley's books for her because Kayley's wrist was still sprained.

She wasn't looking where she was going, so she tripped and fell, twisting her ankle. Now they were even.

Not only that, but when Taylor fell, she got the crowd's applause and teasing, instead of Alexis, who made it across the cafeteria without dropping her lunch tray for the first time in days.

When classes let out, I headed to the gym, as promised, to meet Cassidy and talk to Ms. Throgfeld about joining cheer mid-season. I didn't think she'd take me, so it wasn't that much of a risk to appear that I was willing. It was a gesture. Maybe a risky one, if Ms. Throgfeld took me up on it right there on the spot, but I was having one of my brave moments.

Besides, I didn't think Ms. Throgfeld would do that. She wasn't that spontaneous of a person. Anyone who had turned her back on cheer the way I had didn't count for much in Ms. Throgfeld's book.

It took a minute after I walked in for Cassidy to notice me and come over.

"Wow. You're really *here*," she said, looking slightly uncomfortable. She glanced over at the seventh and eighth graders who were working out without her.

"I said I would. I'll try it, anyway." I shrugged. "If you guys really need me."

"Yeah, well. Your skills are probably not up to par at all," said Cassidy.

I smiled. The old-new Cassidy was back. "I know. I'll work extra hard, though."

"Hey, Ms. Throgfeld! Madison wants to be the bottom

of the pyramid!" She turned to me. "You don't mind, right?"

I saw Ms. Throgfeld looking over at the two of us, forehead creased in confusion.

Maybe, when I was desperate to be friends again, at the beginning of the year, I would have jumped at the chance to be the bottom of the pyramid, to do whatever Cassidy wanted. But I wasn't really feeling like that anymore. We were going in different directions. That was the way it would be from now on. Cheer wasn't "me" anymore, it was her. I was okay with that. I didn't have to put myself in a low, painful, pyramid-supporting position anymore, even if Alexis and I were the same, perfectly matched height.

"Actually, I'm not sure this is such a good idea, me going back on cheer," I said. "My skills are really pretty rusty. And I doubt Ms. Throgfeld wants me," I whispered. "She's not exactly running over to welcome me back."

"Well, that's true. But at the bottom of the pyramid, no one would see you—at least not until you got your skills back up to par."

I smiled again. As long as she could insult me, without maybe meaning to, she was still Cassidy, and I was still me. That was actually a good sign. "I don't know. I'd better not risk it. I mean, what if I couldn't support you? You need good support, remember?" I asked, referring to the Macy's incident last year, when we were still friends.

She laughed. "God. Don't ever tell anyone about that. Ever."

"I wouldn't," I said, smiling. "So, you go ahead. I'd just end up not being committed enough again."

"Yeah. You're probably right. You really aren't good at commitment these days," she said.

"I'm not?" I asked.

"Besides, everyone on cheer has long hair, which means you totally wouldn't fit in. You'd look really weird, actually. Plus, your coolness factor is still, you know. Questionable." She straightened her ponytail and dashed back over to the group.

Cassidy had insulted me to my face. Things were definitely getting back to normal. Or at least, the new normal.

"Madison? Is there something you need to tell me?" asked Ms. Throgfeld, jogging over to me as I headed for the door.

"No, not really. Sorry if I bothered practice."

"Always nice to see you. Don't be a stranger!" the coach called after me as I left the gym and hurried down the hall to the after-school club room.

I could hear a commotion as I got closer. People were arguing in loud voices, and as I entered the room, Olivia was standing with her back to the whiteboard, as if she wished she could back up even farther. I saw a pile of discarded handmade Endangered Animals Club T-shirts on the table in front of her.

"The ink ran!" one eighth-grade girl was yelling

at Olivia. "And it ruined like ten other shirts of mine."

"I want a refund!" her friend said.

"I've already given back all the refunds I can today!" said Olivia. "What do you think, I carry around hundreds of dollars with me?"

"You should," a boy said. "It's our money and we want it back."

I felt like telling them all sales were final, but I didn't want a mob scene on our hands. Instead, I stepped forward and pulled a notebook out of my backpack. "We already put the money into the bank," I said. "We'll return it, but for the rest of today, we're just taking names. We'll give you each an I.O.U."

Everyone groaned but eventually got in line, and Olivia and I sat there and handed out I.O.U. slips for about half an hour.

Finally we'd handed out our last I.O.U., and in return, we had a hundred streaked, ruined T-shirts to deal with instead.

"Oh, man," Olivia groaned. "We blew it."

I smiled, shaking my head. "No, you don't understand. This is great. This is fabulous. We're back to being nobodies. That means the meanicure worked!"

"Well, good, because the shirts definitely didn't," said Olivia. Then we both started to laugh. "Let's pretend we never started this club," she said.

"Agreed." We found a plastic garbage bag in the supply table, and stuffed it with the ruined shirts. Then we walked out of the room, turned off the light, and closed the door.

Olivia hoisted the garbage bag over her shoulder. "We have to recycle these somehow."

"I'll ask my mom," I promised. "She's picking me up today. She'll know what to do."

Last Things Last

A few days later, there was a cold mid-November breeze coming from the ocean when I walked out of school with Olivia at the end of the day. I tugged my hat down over my ears, and pulled up my collar.

"Look at this." Olivia waved a piece of paper in the frigid air as we waited for Taylor to meet us out front. "Cameron left a note in my locker. Can you believe this?"

"Seriously? What kind of note?" I asked.

She began to read it aloud. "'Olivia, when are you going to do the update again? Other people are so normal and boring. See you around—Cameron,'" she read.

I smiled, because it sounded like he might sort of *like* Olivia. Who was, of course, oblivious.

"He misses you!" I said. "What's wrong with that? Maybe he likes you."

"And maybe he's an obnoxious pinhead. I wish he'd just leave me alone!" Olivia held the note up in front of her and ripped it in half, and then tore it in half again. She tossed the pieces into the air, and the wind lifted them up in a swirl, sending them down the street.

My eyes widened. I think I gasped. "You didn't just do that, Oblivia."

"Do what?" she asked.

"Tear up somebody's name and send it flying off into the universe!" I said.

"Oh. I guess I did. Why?" She looked at me. "What are you so worried about?"

"One, you littered. Two, we just got things back to normal. And now you go and start up something else?" I started running, trying to grab the scraps of paper swirling around in the air. I couldn't let Cameron fly away and end up lying on the street, or in a storm drain, or even worse, drowning in the Atlantic. That could be bad—very bad—for our brand-new and improved karma. It would sink to the bottom of the ocean.

I could only find half of them. "Here. Keep these," I told Olivia, panting. "Put them in your pocket, right now."

"Why?"

"Because we have bad luck when we do stuff like this. Or have you forgotten already? Oh, look—there's another one!" I raced after another scrap and held it up. "I got the N! I got it!"

"Madison? Madison!" Olivia yelled to get my attention. "I think you're one of those people who's going, like, slowly insane."

I put my hands on my hips and was about to yell at her when I realized how crazy I must look, scrounging for litter on the street. We started to laugh, but kept jumping around trying to get the scraps of paper before they blew into oblivion.

"OMG, what happened to you guys?" Taylor said, when she came out and saw us. "Leave you alone for two minutes and you both go crazy."

Cassidy, Alexis, and Kayley passed by while we were all still cracking up and trying to grab the remaining scraps blowing around in the breeze. They didn't say anything, just shook their heads and kept walking.

But then it was like they couldn't help themselves. Cassidy suddenly turned around and said, "Since when is it an after-school sport to catch paper?"

"Don't tell me, this is one of your new little activities," said Alexis. "The paper recycling club."

Same old, same old, I thought. We were acting silly, and they were making fun of us. But then I thought, maybe it doesn't have to go back to being exactly the way it was before. Things could change, even if people didn't . . . right?

"You know what? I'd rather recycle paper than outfits," I said. "Didn't you guys wear the same exact thing *last* Monday?"

"Right. As if we would," Kayley scoffed.

But I could see Cassidy thinking about it, and looking a little uncomfortable. "We have to go," she said suddenly. "We have more important things to do than stand around collecting—"

Suddenly one of the scraps of paper blew right

into her face. "Here." Cassidy handed me the "me" from Cameron's name. "Don't say I never gave you anything."

"I wouldn't," I said. "Hey, how come your nails look better than mine? We got the same thing."

She shrugged. "I guess I just take better care of myself."

"Maybe," I agreed, checking out my own chipped polish. "Maybe it's time I started doing that, too."

"Well, we're going to the mall. See you." Cassidy gave a little wave and followed Kayley and Alexis across the school parking lot to Alexis's mom's waiting minivan.

"We have important things to do, too!" I said. "For instance . . ." I looked at Olivia and Taylor. "What *are* we going to do this afternoon?"

"I don't know," said Olivia. "How about if we go get some fries."

"Okay, but you missed your bus. Is your mom coming to pick you up?" I asked.

"No. Wow. I guess I should have planned better, huh?" said Olivia.

"Then I guess you'll have to ride on my handlebars," said Taylor.

"Oh, no. You won't even be able to see if I do that," said Olivia. "No. I'll pedal, *you* ride. I'm a lot taller."

"I'll pedal," said Taylor. "It's my bike. My ankle just got better. I can't risk getting injured again."

"And I can?" said Olivia, laughing.

"Anyway, the seat would be too low for you."

"I'll raise it," said Olivia.

"You don't know how," Taylor said.

"You're not strong enough to pedal both of us."

"Hello? Have you seen my leg muscles?"

They kept on like that, arguing the whole way to the bike rack. I unlocked my bike and slid it out from the metal rack, leaning it on its kickstand while I stuffed the U-lock into my backpack. "You guys realize . . . we could be there by now," I said.

"So what are we waiting for?" Olivia asked. Without asking, she grabbed *my* bike, hopped onto it, and started riding away, laughing. "See you at the Whale!" she called over her shoulder.

"My bike!" I yelled. "I can't believe she just did that," I said to Taylor.

"If she wasn't so nice, and so ditzy that she didn't have another way home, I think I'd hate her right now," Taylor muttered as she pulled on her helmet. "So. Like I said to Olivia, I'll pedal. Where do you want to sit? Front or back?"

I felt one of those flashes of bravery that were sometimes misguided, but sometimes right on the money. "I'll take the handlebars," I said, carefully perching on the front of her bike, then lifting my feet up off the ground.

What was the worst that could happen?

Wait. Don't answer that.

Acknowledgments

I am extremely grateful to Ruth Katcher for her brilliant, insightful editing, and to my agent, Jill Grinberg, for her wisdom and guidance.

Thanks, as always, to my family for their support, and for understanding the need to keep ice-cream sandwiches stocked in our freezer at all times.

And I couldn't have written this without my friends and the members of CS who inspired me. You shall remain nameless, don't worry.

(Same goes for you mean girls.)

Catherine Clark is the author of *Wish You Were Here, Better Latte Than Never,* and many other books for young readers. She has never tried and does not endorse the methods in this book, but she had a close group of friends in seventh grade and remembers it was always two against one. She is also terrible at applying nail polish.

She lives in Meaneapolis—er, that's Minneapolis— with her husband and daughter. Visit her online at www.catherineclark.com.